William Norris

Miss Wentworth's idea

A Novel. Vol. 1

William Norris

Miss Wentworth's idea
A Novel. Vol. 1

ISBN/EAN: 9783337273712

Printed in Europe, USA, Canada, Australia, Japan

Cover: Foto ©Andreas Hilbeck / pixelio.de

More available books at **www.hansebooks.com**

MISS WENTWORTH'S IDEA.

MISS WENTWORTH'S IDEA.

A NOVEL.

BY

W. E. NORRIS,

AUTHOR OF

"MATRIMONY," "MY FRIEND JIM," "THE ROGUE,"
"A BACHELOR'S BLUNDER," ETC.

LONDON:
WARD & DOWNEY
12, YORK STREET, COVENT GARDEN, W.C.
1891.

PRINTED BY
KELLY AND CO., GATE STREET, LINCOLN'S INN FIELDS, W.C.,
AND KINGSTON-ON-THAMES.

CONTENTS.

MISS WENTWORTH'S IDEA.

MISS WENTWORTH'S IDEA.

CHAPTER I.

ONE dark afternoon, in the depth of the dark
and dreary London winter, Miss Wentworth
was toasting her toes before the drawing-room
fire of her brother's house in Upper Brook
Street, which was also her house, inasmuch as
it was her home, and as she paid the half of the
rent, rates and taxes due in respect thereof.
There were plenty of people who admired Miss
Wentworth immensely; and although her nose
was certainly too short and her mouth rather
too large, it cannot be said that their admiration

was misplaced. For she had that look of breeding which is more than a sufficient substitute for beauty ; added to which, her large grey eyes placed her above any need for substitutes. The possession of iron-grey eyes and long dark eyelashes should be enough to meet all ordinary requirements, and if Miss Wentworth's requirements were not ordinary that was only because, like the generality of us, she did not know when she was well off.

At this moment the expression of her face denoted weariness and dissatisfaction. It may be conceded that she was too rich and too good-looking to be dissatisfied ; but perhaps she had some right to be weary, since she was doing nothing, and of all methods of killing time that is, no doubt, the most wearisome. On the other hand, she might have pleaded that she was doing nothing for the excellent reason that she had nothing to do. The dinner had been ordered long ago ; she had paid some visits, she had written a few letters, she had just had her tea, and if there was any better way of spending the next three hours than gazing at the fire and wishing she was somebody else, it was her misfortune to be unacquainted with it. The afternoon post had brought her half-a-dozen notes of a more or less uninteresting description, and these lay upon the tea-table beside her, with the exception of the last that she had chanced to open, which she was still holding between her finger and thumb. It was merely a printed intimation, endorsed with the compliments of the Vicar of the parish, to the effect that the Rev. the Hon. Ernest Compton would preach on the following evening, on behalf of the Society of S. Francis, the good work of which was necessarily restricted owing to lack of funds.

1*

Miss Wentworth was idly wondering what was meant by the Society of S. Francis, who its reverend and honourable supporter might be, and whether he was likely, in the course of his sermon, to supply any fresh notions to a young woman who was quite as urgently in need of a mission in life as he could be of money, when the butler announced "Lady Morecambe."

"You, of all people!" she exclaimed, starting up and embracing the very smartly dressed little lady who bore that title. "What in the world has brought you up to London, Harriet?"

Lady Morecambe was no longer very young and had never been very pretty; yet the general effect of her was a near approach to prettiness. Perhaps she or her dressmaker knew how to make the most of her charms; perhaps now that her hair was streaked with

grey, she had reached an age at which regularity
of feature ceases to be a matter of importance ;
or, perhaps, her bright, alert little face would
have been pleasant to look upon at any time of
life.

" Oh, shopping," she said, in answer to Miss
Wentworth's question. " I don't know how it
is that whenever I find it absolutely essential to
buy a score of things it is sure to be on a
Saturday. However, I have contrived to get
through all my jobs this time by rising long
before the lark and coming up by the early
express ; and now, if you please, I should like a
cup of tea."

" Of course, you shall have your tea,"
answered Miss Wentworth, ringing the bell ;
" but how about dinner? And at what hour do
you expect to reach home again ? "

"Good gracious me ! you don't suppose I am
going back to-night, do you ? I have arranged

a little party to dine somewhere or other this evening and go to the theatre afterwards, and to-morrow I propose to spend a quiet Sunday all by myself in Eaton Square. The one great advantage of having a London house is that it gives one an excuse for running up like this every now and then."

"Well," remarked Miss Wentworth, laughing, "you are a tolerably unceremonious kind of hostess, I must say! What about the large party that you have left at Morecambe? And what about Sylvia, who is supposed to be under your especial care?"

"Sylvia will be all right," answered Lady Morecambe; "you needn't distress yourself about her. There are lots of old women in the house who will feel it their duty to keep a stern eye upon her in my absence, and see that she doesn't get into mischief. As for my other guests, Morecambe is quite capable of looking after them. They were kind enough to say with one consent that they would gladly excuse me when I told them I wanted to pay a flying visit to London in order to hear Ernest Compton preach."

"You said you had come up to do shopping. But who is this Mr. Compton, and what does he mean by his Society of S. Francis? I have just had a notice about him from my Vicar."

"The idea of a Churchy person like you never having heard of Ernest Compton! Well, my dear, he is simply the finest preacher living, and so you will think when you have listened to him. We'll go to church together to-morrow evening, and if he doesn't make you resolve to renounce the pomps and vanities of this wicked world forthwith I shall be very much surprised. He invariably produces that effect upon me, I know."

" Still you don't seem to have done it yet."

" Well, no ; because, you see, *la nuit porte conseil,* and there are rather serious difficulties in the way of my retiring from the world just at present. Nevertheless, I am sure he does me an immense deal of good, besides emptying my purse. Don't take more than you can afford to lose with you, for it is quite certain that the Society of S. Francis will get all you have about you. I can't tell you exactly what the Society of S. Francis is ; but I believe it consists of enthusiastic persons who have adopted a sort of system of Christian socialism or social Christianity. They all live together in a great red-brick building near Soho Square, and devote themselves to good works and the gradual regeneration of mankind. One can't help admiring them ; but perhaps one may be allowed to think twice or three times before imitating them. To resign all one's earthly goods is rather a strong measure. It leaves no room for repentance, you see—and I am so given to repenting."

" Has Mr. Compton resigned all his earthly goods ? " inquired Miss Wentworth.

Lady Morecambe shrugged her shoulders. " Yes, I believe so," she answered. " It sounds an idiotic thing to do ; but perhaps in his case it doesn't so very much matter, for he has never married and never will. He is a connection of ours, a son of old Lord Chepstow, who strongly disapproves of his ways of going on—if that signifies. But really it is impossible to judge Ernest by ordinary standards ; he isn't a man, he is a priest—or rather a saint—like that Francis of Assisi after whom he has named his society."

" I don't think I remember exactly what S. Francis of Assisi did," observed Miss Wentworth, musingly.

"Nor do I, except that he preached to the birds and suggested that lovely music to Lizst; but no doubt he did some rather more practical things than that. I fancy that he was a species of communist, and that his communism consisted chiefly in sacrificing himself for his neighbours, otherwise Ernest Compton wouldn't revere his memory so much."

People who are better acquainted with the history of S. Francis of Assisi than Lady Morecambe or Miss Wentworth could pretend to be will be aware that the communism which he advocated applied only to the monastic order established by him, and will surmise that no sane follower of his in the nineteenth century would seek to make his precepts of universal application. Now, the Rev. Ernest Compton was eminently sane, although his claim to be so considered was not admitted by all his friends. He was, no doubt, something of an enthusiast, and from the first he had cast in his lot with the advanced section of the High Church party ; but it was rather owing to the force of circumstances than to intention that he had become a popular and fashionable preacher. His own inclination would have led him to undertake mission work amongst the heathen or in the East End of London in preference to rousing the somewhat sluggish and ephemeral emotions of smart ladies ; but he was willing to do whatever his special capabilities might seem to fit him best for, and the remarkable success which had attended his sermons during the preceding season had convinced him that for the present, at all events, it was his duty to remain where he was. He had the knack of touching these people and moving them to intermittent acts of benevolence.

Personally, he had little liking or respect for them, nor was any one more thoroughly aware

than he that from nine out of ten of them the
most he would ever get would be money; yet,
since money is of supreme importance, he felt
bound to obtain it when and where he could,
and every now and then his zeal was refreshed
by the admission of some unexpected adherent
into the select band of which he was the leader.
Many men spoke of him as a humbug ; many
women described him as a saint ; in reality, he
was an honest, clear-headed man, struggling
hard to bring the principles of Christianity into
line with the practice of the nations which
profess that faith, and doing his little utmost
to subvert the latter when he found it hope-
lessly at variance with the former.   After
that, it will surprise nobody to hear that at
the age of five-and-forty his hair was almost
white.

Nevertheless, this circumstance came as something of a surprise to Miss Wentworth, who had

been given to understand that he was still in the prime of life, and who, when she saw him, was disposed to think that she had been brought to church under false pretences. Throughout the service she and her companion had been troubled with apprehensions upon that point, for Mr. Compton had not taken his place among the officiating clergy; but while the concluding hymn was being sung, this grey-headed little man had emerged from the vestry and ascended into the pulpit with quick steps, and a nod from Lady Morecambe, in response to Miss Went-worth's inquiring glance, signified to the latter that it was all right.

The little grey-headed man took a swift preliminary look round the building, which enabled such of his hearers as had not seen him before to note that his eyes were black and piercing. In other respects his face could scarcely be called remarkable. It was clean-shaven and somewhat stern in expression ; he had the slightly prominent cheekbones and the thin-lipped mouth of an ascetic; his nose was insignificant, and his forehead neither broad nor high—his countenance, in short, was of that priestly type which is repeated again and again, with trifling variations, throughout Christendom.   He crossed himself rapidly, murmured a few scarcely audible words, and then, as the congregation resumed their seats, gave out his text in a voice which, though low in pitch, was penetrating: "For what doth the Lord thy God require of thee but to do justice and to love mercy and to walk humbly with thy God ? "

His exordium was not striking.   He began, as probably most people, preaching from such text, would have begun, by pointing out the apparent modesty of the standard set up, and that, at least as regarded the first two of its precepts, most of us would claim to have fulfilled them ; since, ready though we are to accuse ourselves of all manner of sins, very few of us are disposed to plead guilty to a charge of injustice or cruelty. Then, by a few telling examples, some of which he read from a newspaper of the previous day, he contrasted human justice with Divine. Human justice, existing above and before all things for the protection of the sacred rights of property, punishing paltry thefts with tremendous penalties and allowing some of the worst of criminals to go free, does not even pretend to take its stand upon Christian doctrine. Its justification is its alleged necessity, and if Christianity cannot be made to fit in with it, so much the worse for Christianity.

"It may," said the preacher, "be necessary for the preservation of society that our laws should remain unaltered. I do not deny this ;

I only submit that we cannot be certain of it, because no trial has ever been given to a more merciful system; and it is as well to remember that, whereas, not so many years ago, it was deemed necessary to put men to death for sheep-stealing, sheep have not been stolen in greater numbers since the abolition of capital punishment for that offence. But the question for us, as individuals, is whether we have any right at all to describe ourselves as followers of Christ, so long as we either refuse to obey his distinct commands or endeavour to place a strained interpretation upon them."

It was from this point that he became more animated, and that his eloquence began to carry his hearers along with him.

Anybody can show the miserable inadequacy of our notions and practice with regard to justice and mercy; not a few can do it convincingly; but only a true orator can overcome that stolid barrier of common sense behind which the Anglo-Saxon race is wont to entrench itself and sway a British audience at his will. It is true that no audience in the world is quite so unreasoning as a British audience when once that feat has been accomplished.

Miss Wentworth, to whom common sense and logic and hard facts had never presented themselves in any attractive guise, was conquered without the least difficulty. At last—so it seemed to her—she had found one whose guidance she could follow implicitly and confidently. This fiery little man, whose gestures were so spontaneous, whose voice was so thrilling and sympathetic, and whose insight into the workings of the human heart was so keen, at least meant every word that he said— there could be no doubt about that. And he was not tender with those who listened to him;

he did not spare their little weaknesses and vanities and hypocrisies, with which he seemed to be as well acquainted as any cynical man of the world could be; and when he called upon them to act for the future more in accordance with their nominal professions, he contrived to frame that well-worn appeal in such a way as to give it a certain air of novelty. What was, perhaps, the cleverest part of his discourse—that in which he indicated the obvious duty of humility, and dwelt ironically upon the arrogant assumptions of science and the fantastic experiments of those who would fain set up a religion of Christianity without Christ—scarcely touched Miss Wentworth, for her faith had always remained unshaken; but she was fairly carried away by what she believed to be the truth of his conceptions with regard to the Christian life, and he had been speaking for upwards of half an hour before she remembered that, so far, he had said nothing at all about the society of S. Francis.

But, indeed, he had only a few words to say upon that subject, and he said them in a quiet and lowered voice, after the pause which succeeded his peroration. Of the rules and aims of that confraternity he did not, he said, propose to speak. Many members of the congregation were already acquainted with these ; those who were not could easily obtain information, and they were not, he was aware, such as to command universal approval. " But whether you approve or disapprove of the vows which we have chosen to take upon ourselves, whether you set us down as visionaries or fools, whether you imagine that we are trying to revive monasticism, or whether you suspect that the exaggerated self-consciousness of the age is our real motive for separating ourselves from our neighbours, you cannot possibly dis-

2*

approve of our work. And it is only on behalf of our work that I am here to ask for
your alms."

He then gave a brief and rapid account of
what had been accomplished during the year
which was drawing to its close. They had a
children's hospital which was full to overflowing,
and required enlargement; they had trained
sick nurses ; they had sent out missionaries to
all quarters of the globe; they had worked
among the poor in many London and provincial
parishes, and their help had been gratefully
accepted by the clergy belonging to all the
various schools which are included in the
Church of England. He was not, therefore,
asking them to support any sect or denomina-
tion, but simply to give of their superfluity to
those whose claims had never been, because they
never could be, disputed. The request was not
an impassioned one ; but, doubtless, the speaker,

who knew whom he was addressing, knew also
that it would be responded to. For, indeed,
when you have been made to feel thoroughly
ashamed of yourself, it is some comfort to think
that you can in a measure recover your self-
esteem by so easy a process as emptying your
pocket.

Miss Wentworth earned such satisfaction
as was to be obtained from the emptying of
her pocket, but did not find it sufficient for her.

"Does the society of S. Francis consist only
of men?" she asked Lady Morecambe, as they
drove away, interrupting her companion's un-
stinting praises of the sermon which they had
just heard.

"Oh, dear, no!" answered Lady Morecambe,
laughing; "didn't he tell you that it was a part
of their work to train nurses? Are you thinking of joining them, Muriel? That would be
just like you."

"I don't know whether it would be like me," answered Miss Wentworth, slowly; "but it would be what I should like. Don't you ever wish to be of *some* use in the world?"

"I flatter myself that I am of considerable use, and I should have thought that you, too, were not without utility. However, you may safely offer yourself and your fortune to Ernest Compton; for, unless I am greatly mistaken, he won't accept either. You see, my dear, he happens to be a gentleman."

"I don't understand," said Miss Wentworth.

"That only shows how stupid some clever people may be. I, of course, am only a goose; yet I have intelligence enough to perceive that there are certain offers which a gentleman can't accept. I am glad he has made you lose your head, though. He always affects me in that way—only I get over it the next day, you know."

CHAPTER II.

WHEN Miss Wentworth reached home, she went straight into her brother's study; for she felt that she owed him an apology. Mr. Wentworth did not object to dining occasionally at his club —but he objected very strongly to dining alone ; and as she had unfortunately forgotten to tell him that she was going to church that evening, she had been obliged to leave a note for him, announcing her intention.

" I hope you have had your dinner all right, James ? " she said.

" As it is now nearly a quarter-past nine," answered the sandy-haired, middle-aged man, who was smoking his cigar in an easy chair, before the fire, " I need hardly tell you that I have had my dinner. I believe it was more or less all right, although I do wish that your cook had the same love for new ideas as you have. But, perhaps, that would be rather too much to expect. Well, how do you like the Anglican monk? "

" He isn't a monk," answered Miss Wentworth, advancing to the fireside and drawing off her gloves, " he looked just like any other parson. But he didn't talk like the others. Oh, James, he was magnificent! I wish you could have heard him ! "

" If he is magnificent, I wish I could ; and if he will come here some day and preach to me I shall be delighted to listen to anything that he may have to say ; but never yet have I met a parson who could draw me to such an abominably uncomfortable thing as an evening service."

" You wouldn't have thought about that ; you wouldn't have known whether you were comfortable or not. At least, he would have given you such mental discomfort that you would have forgotten everything else."

" Ah, I don't like mental discomfort," observed Mr. Wentworth, tranquilly ; "you, of course, do. *Des goûts et des couleurs !* I've heard all about the man, you know. He has started some kind of self-denying Order, with vows of poverty and celibacy and all the rest of it, and he has chucked every penny that he possesses into his scheme. Admirable ; but, shall we say a trifle asinine ? Because, you see, that sort of thing is quite out of date, and can't last."

" I don't see it at all," Miss Wentworth declared.

" No, you wouldn't. Well, so long as it amuses you and the other ladies, and so long as

you don't go to the length of parting with all
your worldly goods for an idea, your monk
serves his purpose, no doubt.   I can well
imagine how edified Lady Morecambe must be
by him."

Mr. Wentworth laughed softly to himself as
he watched the smoke from his cigar rising
towards the ceiling.   It was his habit to laugh
at most people and things, and he had always
found that this mental attitude of his kept him
in tolerably good health and spirits.   He was
only Muriel Wentworth's half-brother, and was
more than twenty years older than she.   He
was also, although a well-to-do man, consider-
ably poorer ; for his stepmother, who had had a
large fortune, had bequeathed the whole of it
to her only child.   As this lady had died about
the same time that he himself had been left a
widower, it had seemed natural that Muriel
should make her home with him, and he had

very cordially agreed to that arrangement. For one thing, it was lucrative, because she could very well afford to defray half the expenses of the household and the cost of a carriage; and for another, it ensured him the services of a tolerably experienced housekeeper, which his daughter Sylvia, who was only just out of the schoolroom, could have no pretension to be. The only trouble was the probability, which might almost be regarded as a certainty, that Muriel would ere long marry somebody or other.

Muriel, however, notwithstanding certain advantageous offers, had not as yet seen fit to marry anybody; and if she appeared to be as satisfied with the existing state of things as Mr. Wentworth was, that was only because she was of a somewhat reticent temperament. In reality she was thoroughly dissatisfied. She had not that intense craving for the pleasures of this

life which is common among young people, and
she was perhaps rather abnormally alive to its
duties and responsibilities.   It was a duty, of
course, to look after her brother's servants for
him, and to study cookery-books on his behalf ;
it was also a duty to act in some sort of way as a
mother to Sylvia, who was disposed to be wilful
and imprudent in her dealings with young men ;
but these things did not quite suffice to fulfil
the requirements of a modest ambition.   There
was no lack of good-natured matrons, such as
Lady Morecambe, at whose country house the
girl was now staying, to chaperon Sylvia ; while
as for James, nothing was more likely than that
he would some day take to himself a second wife.
Muriel Wentworth wanted to be of some service
to humanity at large ; she could not believe that
she had been created for the sole purpose of
ordering the dinner and the carriage, and she
was unable, upon mature reflection, to see why

the fact of Mr. Compton's being a gentleman should preclude him from accepting at least a part of the money which she did not know how to spend, and providing her, in return, with the occupation of which she stood so sorely in need.

On the following morning, therefore, she summoned up courage to write a long letter to the preacher whose eloquence had so profoundly impressed her. She laid her case before him, she explained what her wishes were, and she begged him to take her word for it that she was not acting upon the mere impulse of the moment. She was not, she admitted, free from all doubt as to the manner in which she ought to dispose of her money, but she thought that the obstacles which seemed to stand in the way of her devoting it to charitable purposes were not insuperable. In any case, she had no one whose advice she could ask upon such a subject, and she ventured to hope that he would not refuse her his. Could he find time to come and see her any afternoon after five o'clock?

It was not without trepidation that she posted this appeal to a total stranger ; yet when she remembered the kindly and sympathetic inflections which his voice had taken during certain passages of his discourse, she felt sure that he would understand what she had not expressed so well as she could have wished, and that he would give her an opportunity of stating her views with more precision by word of mouth. Had she been better acquainted with Mr. Compton she would have known that it was a very common thing with him to receive letters from ladies who had been moved to repentance by his sermons, and that such experiences were not greatly to his taste. Not being aware of this, she felt a good deal snubbed when the following rather curt and formal reply reached her by return of post :—

"Madam,—I am much occupied just now, but I will endeavour to call upon you on Thursday next, as you request, at the hour which you mention.—Faithfully yours, ERNEST COMPTON."

Well, of course, these few cold words made her wish that she had been less precipitate and less confidential; perhaps also—for human nature is weak—they may have made her wish for a chance of retaliating upon her reverend and honourable correspondent. But in any case it was evident that she could not now draw back; nor, in truth, after calm consideration, did she desire to do so. After all, he was entitled to doubt her sincerity; it was for her to convince him that she was both

serious and resolute. This she quite hoped
that she would be able to do; so she carefully rehearsed in advance the conversation
which she intended to hold with him, and
received him in a cold and self-possessed
manner when he duly made his appearance
at the appointed hour.

He, on his side, was perfectly at his ease. He
shook hands, accepted her offer of a cup of tea,
and began to talk commonplaces just like any
ordinary visitor. Once or twice, to be sure, she
found those searching black eyes of his fixed
upon her; but apparently they did not discover
anything interesting, for he continued to speak
about Lady Morecambe and the county ball
which she was about to patronise, as though
such topics were the ones most likely to suit his
companion. It was not without difficulty, and
not until he had been sitting beside her for a
quarter of an hour, that Muriel contrived to

drag S. Francis of Assisi in by the head and shoulders.

"Oh, well," said Mr. Compton, laughing half-apologetically, "a society must have some name, you know, and it so happens that of all the saints, S. Francis of Assisi is the one for whom I have the greatest personal veneration. I think, too, that we may describe ourselves as to some extent following in his footsteps. We see, at any rate, what nobody can help seeing, that after nineteen centuries Christianity has failed to establish itself as the religion of the world, and we hold, rightly or wrongly, that this is because the world has never really practised Christianity. We neither pretend nor expect to revolutionise society ; only we think it incumbent upon us to make our own microscopic efforts in what we believe to be the right direction. For the rest, our charitable work is such as you or any other outsider may safely subscribe to. It is not

necessary to be a Christian in order to recognise
the duty of clothing the naked, feeding the
hungry, and visiting the sick."

"But I don't want to be an outsider; I want
to join you," Muriel declared boldly. "I fully
agree with you that Christianity has never had
a fair trial ; I don't believe that criminals ought
to be punished, or that war ought to exist, or
that a few of us ought to be rich while the
enormous majority are poor ; and I wish, if you
will allow me, to give myself and such money
as I have in aid of what you call your microscopic efforts."

"Oh, but I'm afraid I can't allow you,"
answered Mr. Compton, shaking his head and
laughing again, "we don't accept recruits like
that from one moment to another. You have
read Tolstoï, perhaps?"

"Well, yes," Muriel confessed, a little re-
luctantly; "why do you ask?"

" I thought it not improbable that you had. Tolstoï may fairly claim to be respected ; but as for imitating him, that is another affair. One must make sure, in the first place, that one has the courage of one's opinions ; and, in the second, that one is quite free to act upon them. I gathered from your letter that you did not consider yourself wholly free from family obligations."

" The question is whether the obligations are real or not, and that is just what I wished to consult you about. My half-brother, as I told you, is a widower who may marry again ; in anticipation of that, I should like to make some provision for my niece, and I suppose I could do so, could I not ? Even then I should not come to you by any means empty-handed."

" Oh, we should be satisfied with the residue of your fortune, Miss Wentworth. But don't you think it possible that you have duties ready

3*

to your hand which may very well content you for some years to come? And don't you— pardon me—think that you may look at the world from an altogether different point of view a few years hence?"

" I think," answered Muriel, that I am old enough to know my own mind ; but of course I understand your feeling conscientiously bound to throw cold water over me. I must try to persuade you that that is not necessary, and that I am not exactly the hysterical young woman whom you evidently take me for."

She tried accordingly, and if she was not absolutely convincing, she was at least earnest and honest. For so much Mr. Compton probably gave her credit, for it was in a graver and kindlier tone than he had hitherto adopted that he delivered the judgment for which she paused.

" My dear young lady," said he, " I doubt

neither your zeal nor your convictions; but I am sure your own good sense will tell you how impossible it would be for me to take your money at present, except in the form of some comparatively trifling annual subscription. To put it upon no higher grounds, I really cannot afford to rob you. What would the newspapers say about me and my unhappy Society if it transpired that we had induced a very young lady with very large means to join us?"

"And yet you talk of having the courage of your opinions! Is one to be deterred from doing what is right by fear of ignorant gossip or slander?"

"Oh, I hope not; but you see, Miss Wentworth, it hasn't exactly been proved to demonstration that you would be right in giving us all your possessions, or that we should be right in taking them. And since it is our aim to influence public opinion as far as our abilities will allow us to do so, we must needs show a little respect for it. However, as I said before, we won't refuse a small subscription."

Muriel bit her lips. "It seems to me," said she, "that, considering what your professions are, you are singularly selfish. Of course I will gladly give you a subscription; but you know very well that permission to become a subscriber was not what I asked for. I subscribe to plenty of charities already, and I could easily subscribe to plenty more. What I want is personal employment in the service of my fellow-creatures, and that you won't give me, because you are afraid lest people should accuse you of greed or undue influence, or something of that kind."

"I daresay I can find employment for you if you wish it," answered Mr. Compton, "although I should think you ought to have no difficulty in finding it for yourself. As regards the charge of

selfishness, surely—supposing that I were rude
enough to do such a thing—I might retort *tu
quoque!* Why are you so eager to throw yourself and your fortune at the heads of your
fellow-creatures? Is it altogether out of a dis-
interested love for them?"

Muriel was angry and offended; but she
flattered herself that self-control enabled her to
conceal these emotions. "You don't believe in
me yet," she observed quietly; "perhaps you
will believe in me some day. I am sorry that
you should be so sceptical; but I daresay experience has made you so." She could not help
adding, "I wish you were a little bit more like
your sermons!"

He smiled, and said that that was a species of
criticism to which all preachers were inured; it
was necessary to use one kind of language to a
mixed assembly and another to individuals. He
could only assure her that it would give him

great pleasure if he were able to assist or advise her in any practical way.

Miss Wentworth was afraid that practical counsels would be of very little comfort to her. Not being an absolute idiot, she was aware that she could follow the precepts of the Church Catechism, live respected, and die more or less lamented ; but, unhappily, that scheme of life did not happen to realise her ideal. Still, she was grateful to Mr. Compton for having sacrificed so much of his valuable time to her, and she hoped that their acquaintance would not cease then and there.

If she thought that little display of dignified ill-temper would take her mentor down a peg or two, she was disappointed. Mr. Compton said what was polite and conventional, and, after thanking her for the bank-notes which she handed to him, withdrew, leaving her with tears of anger as well as of vexation in her eyes. She was very sorry that she had been so silly as to send for him ; she was still more sorry that he should have shown so evident an appreciation of her silliness ; yet, though silenced, she was not discouraged, and she registered an inward vow that Mr. Compton should understand her a little better before he had done with her.

Meanwhile, it was time for her to go and dress for a dinner-party to which she and her brother had been bidden.

If there was one form of entertainment which Mr. Wentworth liked, and Muriel disliked, more than another, it was a dinner-party. Their requirements, probably, were not the same, and, doubtless, his were more easily fulfilled than hers. It was, therefore, with the confident expectation of spending three hours of unrelieved weariness that Miss Wentworth seated herself in the brougham beside her brother, who remarked, cheerfully :

" We shall have some fun this evening."

" Fun!" she ejaculated ; "why should you anticipate that of all things in the world ? "

" Because we are going to meet Mrs. Hill. Doesn't Mrs. Hill amuse you ? "

" Well, not very much," Muriel confessed.

" Ah, poor you! I suppose not. . What a lot of innocent amusement you are deprived of by your morose temperament. You really should try to acquire the knack of being diverted by people who don't mean to be diverting. Believe me, you will find it a solace with advancing years."

" After all, poor Mrs. Hill is a thoroughly kind-hearted woman," Muriel remarked, some-what inconsequently.

' Who denies the kindness of her heart ? Nevertheless, she amuses me without intending it, and so—with the highest possible respect for you—do you, my dear. But then I am a simple

creature ; it doesn't take a great deal to make
me laugh. I would have given a good deal to
be present at your interview with your monastic
friend this afternoon."

"How did you know that I had an interview with him?" inquired Muriel, glad that
the darkness concealed her heightened
colour, for in truth she was rather more
sensitive to ridicule than enthusiastic persons
ought to be.

" I made so bold as to ask Hopkins
whether anybody had called, and he told
me the Reverend Compton had been having
tea with you. Did he come up to your ex-
pectations ? "

" Oh, yes, thank you ; and if you had been
there I don't think you would have found much
to laugh at in him. He takes a very sensible,
commonplace view of life."

" How funny of him ! I suppose he must

have thought that you stood in need of a corrective. Well, I trust you may be led in to dinner to-night by somebody equally interesting."

"There is not the faintest hope of that," answered Muriel, with a sigh.

CHAPTER III.

ONE advantage which a London dinner party possesses over a provincial one is that at the former you never can tell whom you may meet, whereas at the latter there is seldom room for any uncertainty upon the subject. And so a little surprise was in store for Miss Wentworth, who certainly had not expected, on entering the drawing-room, to recognise Mr. Compton among the dozen or so of guests assembled there. But there was no mistaking the grey-headed cleric, and he at once greeted her with a smile and an outstretched hand.

"How very odd that we should meet twice in one day, although we have never met before!"

she exclaimed. "I should have thought you
would have disdained such frivolous entertainments as this."

"Why?" he asked.

She could not think of any adequate reply,
and was conscious of having said a stupid and,
perhaps, a rather impertinent thing, through
sheer lack of sufficient presence of mind to hold
her tongue, but he did not seem to notice her
embarrassment.

"I know no reason why one shouldn't dine
with one's friends if one has the time," he
remarked, after a short pause. "I don't often
dine out, because I haven't the time ; but I am
here this evening in discharge of what may
almost be counted as coming into the cate-
gory of professional duties. Our hostess
gives me a good deal of money, and she
expects me, in return, to show myself at her
house every now and then. That is a kind

of sacrifice which can be made cheerfully enough."

" Yes," agreed Muriel, hesitatingly ; " but isn't it a little undignified ? "

" Oh, I am quite prepared to sacrifice my dignity, such as it is," he answered, laughing. " Perhaps I did that when I laid myself out to be a popular preacher ; but, as you may imagine, I acted from motives which appeared to me to be sufficient. Like a certain famous author, *je prends mon bien où je le trouve ;* I knew from the first that I should not be able to pick and choose."

His tone jarred upon her a little ; he seemed determined to exhibit himself to her as less of a hero than her fancy had painted him, and she could not understand why he should be so perverse. Surely it was beneath him to show himself at dinner-parties as a lion, and—as he had half hinted was the case—to resort to oratorical persuasion which was not spontaneous in order to obtain money. But she was unable, though not unwilling, to say this to him ; for other lady admirers of his were present who claimed his attention, and she was disappointed of her hope that he might be assigned to her as a neighbour at the dinner table. In his stead she was awarded to a certain Colonel Medhurst, who was introduced to her at the last moment, and whom she mentally classified, after a brief scrutiny, as a middle-aged military man of the stereotyped, dull pattern.

Colonel Medhurst was certainly middle-aged, inasmuch as he had passed that fortieth year from which the down-hill road of life may be said to begin ; but he was tall, broad-shouldered and straight-backed ; his blue eyes were as clear as a boy's, and his closely cut brown hair had as yet no threads of grey in it. Every pro-fession leaves its recognisable stamp upon those who have followed it for twenty years, so that the outward appearance of the man was, no doubt, of the stereotyped cavalry pattern ; yet his conversation could not fairly be called dull, as even the fastidious Miss Wentworth had to admit after five minutes. He had just returned from India, he told her, and, owing to various causes, had been away from England for quite an eternity.

"So that I feel as if I were in a strange land," he said, "and everything strikes me as being queer and strange. People's houses aren't in the least like what they used to be ; nor are their dinners ; nor are they themselves, for the matter of that."

" Improved or deteriorated ? " inquired Muriel.

" The furniture has improved, and so have the dinners ; I don't think I am quite so sure about the people. They aren't shy, which I suppose must be counted as an advance, and they are certainly better informed than their predecessors ; only I fancy they are a good deal less domestic than they were in the days of my youth, and that seems to me to be a pity. Of course, I am speaking of the women."

" Oh, yes, that is a matter of course ; one knows that when a man sets to work to criticise the world, it is always the other sex that he falls foul of. You have a comfortable theory that society is what women choose to make it."

" Well, but isn't that a correct theory ? " asked Colonel Medhurst.

" No, I don't think so. Women, as a rule, wish to please you, so they suit themselves to what they imagine to be your tastes. You will hardly go so far as to assert that you ever think of suiting yourselves to ours."

The Colonel, after pondering for a moment, replied that he really couldn't say ; he should think that some men did. "But, you see, it isn't such an easy matter to discover what your tastes are. It is evident enough that you like excitement; but whether you like all the other things that you appear to like seems doubtful. By the way, I saw you in church last Sunday evening, listening to my friend Compton."

"Is Mr. Compton a friend of yours?" asked Muriel, with quickened interest.

"In a certain sense he is, because we were great friends at school; but we have scarcely seen each other since those far-away days; and, although he tells me I am just what I always was, I can't return the compliment. I daresay you will hardly believe it, but Compton was a rather naughty boy."

"I can quite believe it; I don t like good boys," Muriel declared.

"Perhaps you like good men, though, dan if

4*

Compton isn't a good man, I never met one. I won't take upon myself to say that he is wise. Do you know that he was very well off, and that he has given up every penny to this precious Society of his?"

"If that is a foolish thing to do, you will admit at least that it is consistent."

"Certainly it is, and he is worth a thousand of the rest of us. But is this eccentric Society worth the sacrifice of his life and his fortune and his prospects? 'Sell all that thou hast and give to the poor' is what the Roman Catholics call a counsel of perfection; if we all followed it, the business of the world would come to a stand-still."

"There is no danger of our all following it; and he doesn't suggest that we should."

"Oh! I thought he did."

"No; he seems to think that the privilege of being a Christian in reality as well as in name is reserved for the few. And I only wish I were one of the few," added Muriel, sighing.

Colonel Medhurst turned his head so as to study his neighbour's features, and apparently he found the study an agreeable one, for he fairly stared her out of countenance.

"Aren't you one of them?" he inquired at length.

"I am not," she answered, "and I doubt whether I shall ever be allowed to be. Mr. Compton thinks, as I am sure you would if you knew me a little better, that I am only a discontented sort of woman who doesn't know what she wants, and he would no more dream of admitting me into the Society of S. Francis than he would dream of admitting you."

"I don't think he will be requested to admit me, and I hope he will never be requested to admit you, Miss Wentworth. Dear me, you can surely find something better to do with yourself than to become a nun or a Sister of Charity !"

"Most people would say so, of course. The popular notion is that Sisters of Charity should be old maids and poor and ugly ; and we don't believe enough in our religion to give up anything to it, except what we don't want or can't have. But that isn't Mr. Compton's notion, and it isn't mine—if he would only give me credit for having notions worthy of consideration."

"Oh, you have consulted him, then?" Colonel Medhurst began ; but at this moment Muriel had to respond to some remark made by the gentleman who sat on the other side of her, and it was not until dinner was nearly over that he was able to speak to her again.

He re-opened the conversation by asking whether the man opposite with the fair hair and the short, greyish beard wasn't her father.

"I am glad you didn't put that question to him," answered Muriel, "because he wouldn't have liked it. James is my half-brother, and we live together, and I have a niece who is not very many years younger than I am."

"So that he might be your father, after all."

"It would be just possible ; but the suggestion isn't exactly a compliment to him."

"Well, I apologise. And what is the name of the fat lady with the diamonds who is making him laugh so much?"

"She is a Mrs. Hill, and I wish he wouldn't laugh at her quite so unrestrainedly. James has an unfortunate conviction that the people whom he laughs at never by any chance detect him. Sometimes he says things to them that make my blood run cold."

Colonel Medhurst observed gravely that irony was a dangerous weapon. Indeed, he thought so, and had never been able to draw any distinc-

tion between satire and ill-nature. Himself a
very simple and straightforward person, he
valued simplicity and straightforwardness in
others. Therefore he did not think he should
like Mr. Wentworth and was quite sure he
liked that gentleman's sister, though her
opinions probably did not altogether coincide
with his own. He would have tried to elicit a
few more of her opinions from her, if the ladies
had not risen before he had time to begin, and
he thought a great deal about her after their
departure.

She, for her part, was not equally flattering
to him. Colonel Medhurst seemed to be a
pleasant, masculine kind of man; but he obviously belonged to a class of persons with whom
she felt little sympathy, and she dismissed him
from her mind the moment that she turned her
back upon him.

The fat lady with the diamonds made for her,

as she entered the drawing-room, and led her away into a corner, holding her by the hand, and saying:

"My dear Muriel, I want to tell you my news, which I have just been telling to your brother. What do you think? Johnny has been asked to stay with Lord and Lady Morecambe, and he has gone down there this afternoon."

"Yes?" answered Muriel abstractedly; for the confidences of Mrs. Hill seldom interested her.

"Yes, indeed, and I am so glad about it. Isn't it odd that they should have invited him at the same time as dear Sylvia?"

Muriel, after bringing her mind to bear upon the subject, thought it rather odd that they should have invited Johnny Hill at all; but of course she did not give utterance to that reflection.

"I am glad poor Johnny will have somebody he knows to talk to there," she remarked, which comment was only a shade less offensive than her unspoken one.

Mrs. Hill tossed her head. It was a little round head, adorned with little round features, so that it did not bear tossing particularly well. To be effective that kind of gesture requires a hook nose. She said in an affronted tone :

"I can assure you that wherever Johnny goes he meets plenty of people who are willing enough to talk to him. You have known him since his boyhood, and perhaps that is why you don't quite realise that he is now a man. Sylvia realises it, though."

Muriel gazed at her companion in undisguised amazement. "What do you mean?" she asked.

"If you don't know, my dear, you had better ask your brother. He was not in the least

surprised when I told him that I had noticed the
young people's liking for one another. He said
he had noticed it himself; and so, I feel pretty
sure, must Lady Morecambe have done. Considering how kind she has been to Johnny,
do you think I might call upon Lady Morecambe, when she comes up to London? I was
introduced to her once at your house, you
know."

" Perhaps it might be better to let her make
the first advance," answered Muried, successfully
suppressing an inclination to laugh.

" Well, if you think so—although I feel as if
I ought to thank her for having been such a
good friend to Johnny. He is rather needlessly
diffident, poor boy; but I think dear Sylvia will
forgive him for that, don't you? Nowadays
young men are so very seldom given to under-
valuing themselves."

Muriel willingly expressed her disapproval of

the modern young man. She could not possibly say that she considered Johnny Hill's diffidence misplaced, and she inwardly resolved to scold her niece for having given any encouragement to a ridiculous hobbledehoy. Sylvia often deserved a scolding, and sometimes took it in good part ; as for James, he was incorrigible. Of course he had found it amusing to flatter this silly and vulgar woman with hopes of a match which he could never sanction, and of course he would not be in the least ashamed of himself if it were pointed out to him that he had no business to do any such thing.

But what was not a little surprising was that Mr. Wentworth, when taken to task upon the subject, declined to admit that he had been diverting himself at Mrs. Hill's expense. He took Muriel away almost immediately after he and the other men had come upstairs from the dining-room, so that she had no opportunity of saying anything, except good-bye, to Mr. Compton, and as soon as they were once more in the brougham he checked her remonstances by declaring that, in his opinion, Johnny Hill was quite as desirable a son-in-law as another.

"Indeed he is a good deal more desirable than most of them, if you come to that. I suppose he must have at least £5,000 a year of his own, and most likely he will have as much again when his mother dies."

"You only talk like that because you know that it disgusts me, James. You can't suppose for one moment that Sylvia would marry such a booby."

"In the course of a tolerably long and uninterruptedly virtuous life," answered Mr. Wentworth, composedly, "I have known many instances of charming women having married absolute boobies, and I am bound to say that none of them appeared to regret what they had done. If there is one character more than another in which a booby is especially qualified to shine, I suppose it is that of a husband. He is easily pleased, easily pacified, and easily deceived : what more would you have? If, in addition to his other advantages, the booby possesses a large income, he is about as near perfection as anything that one can hope to secure in this wicked world."

" Fortunately, Sylvia won't dream of taking him," observed Muriel, disdaining to make any reply to these cynical sentiments.

" Oh, well, if she won't, she won't ; only don't accuse me of having trifled with Mrs. Hill's maternal solicitude. I can lay my hand upon the front of my shirt and say that nothing would give me greater pleasure than to hear that Sylvia had done so well for herself."

"Then you don't deserve to have a daughter and you have no sort of natural affection."

"Thank you, my dear; the same to you. You are rich, while Sylvia and I are, comparatively speaking, poor; and charity, as I have always been taught, begins at home. I don't expect you to hand over your fortune to us; but when you contemplate casting the whole of it into the lap of the successor of S. Francis I do feel that natural affection is not precisely your strongest point."

This thrust had the effect of silencing Muriel, who could not but acknowledge it to be merited. She did not deem it incumbent upon her to explain that she by no means ignored the claims of her family and that, if she ever joined the Society of S. Francis, it would only be after the fashion of a modern Sapphira.

Meanwhile, Mr. Compton and Colonel Medhurst were walking away together, and the latter was delivering himself of some trenchant criticisms upon the sermon by which certain other persons had been so profoundly impressed.

"It's all very fine, Compton," he was saying, "but there's an unreality about this gospel of yours which rather puts me off. You preach what you don't and can't practise."

"Do I?" asked the other.

"Well, perhaps I have no right to say that; of course I can't know for certain. But this literal forgiving of one's enemies, for instance— how could you reduce such a theory to practice? You'll allow, I take it, that a soldier is bound to fight for his country?"

"Yes, as matters stand at present; but we think that matters stand very badly at present. We should like to see soldiers and all need for soldiers done away with. We might as well say that we should like to see sin and pain and sorrow done away with, you may answer.

Quite so; but our feebleness doesn't excuse us from working towards an end which we can't hope to achieve in full, and at any rate it is well within our power to forgive our personal enemies."

" I don't believe it is within my power to forgive mine," said Medhurst, rather grimly. " At least, there is one man whom it would be nonsense for me to talk about forgiving. I suppose you can guess his name ? "

" No," answered Compton wonderingly; "how should I know ? "

" Well, I thought everybody knew; but I dare say everybody forgets very quickly, and perhaps you can employ your time better than in reading the newspapers. The man whom I mean is my sister's husband, or rather he was her husband until she was compelled to divorce him. Most likely you, with your High Church notions, refuse to recognise such a thing as divorce; yet you would have to acknowledge that, if ever divorce is justifiable, it was so in her case. She bore with him as long as it was possible to bear with him ; she only appealed to the law after he had actually struck her more than once. She never told me a word about it until it was too late for me to interfere ; I was away in India at the time, and I suppose, as she says, my coming home and hammering the brute wouldn't have done much good. Now that I have come home, I find her a miserable, lonely woman, leading a miserable, lonely life through no fault of her own, and still—that's the horrible part of it—secretly worshipping the blackguard to whom it was no punishment at all to be set free from her. You may tell me, if you like, that I am bound to forgive that blackguard ; all I can say in reply is that if you are a mortal man, *you* wouldn't forgive him."

" I can't tell," answered the other, after a few

moments of silence ; "nobody can tell what his capacities are until he has been put to the test. But this much I can say for certain : unless I could forgive such a man from my heart, it wouldn't be possible for me to say my prayers to-night. One reservation, you see, is fatal to the whole scheme of the religion that we profess. It is easy to forgive some people, and immensely difficult to forgive others ; we must take the rough with the smooth, or else acknowledge ourselves beaten."

"If that is so, I acknowledge myself beaten," said Medhurst curtly.

Mr. Compton did not insist ; perhaps he was too experienced a student of his fellow-men to do that.

They marched on, side by side, for some little distance without exchanging another word, and then Medhurst resumed in an altered tone :

"I liked that Miss Wentworth whom I took

5*

in to dinner. She is a very pretty girl, and, I
should think, as good as she is pretty. A great
admirer of yours too, by-the-way."

"I hope you are not smitten with her," said
his friend.

"At my age?—hardly! All the same, I have
no doubt I should be if I were twenty years
younger. She gave me to understand that
you had rather sat upon her; and although, for
her sake, I wasn't very sorry to hear that,
I don't know how you can have reconciled it
with your conscience to drive away such a
promising aspirant. What is your objection to
her?"

"I am scarcely acquainted with her. I met
her for the first time this afternoon; but I saw
enough of her then to see that—in short, that
she is of no use."

"Well, that is just what she complained of;
isn't it?"

"Yes, I believe so. She suffers from a con stitutional ailment which is not only very common, but almost incurable. The people who really want to be of use can always find out ways of being useful without making a fuss about it; Miss Wentworth and the rest of her species prefer to make a fuss. She means well, and I dare say she will turn out an excellent wife in some respects, but the chances are that she will always be discontented, so I don't exactly envy her future husband."

" How like a parson!" exclaimed Colonel Medhurst. " You get into the habit of classifying people, and you are as confident in your own judgments as if you were so many swell physicians."

"What else can you expect of us? We haven't the time to go minutely into individual cases ; only we learn to recognise certain symptoms, just as the swell physicians do. They and we are sometimes wrong ; but we are much more often right."

" Nevertheless, I shall take the liberty of continuing to think that Miss Wentworth is only discontented because she hasn't yet discovered her mission in life."

" Who contradicts you ? The question is whether she will ever discover it. But, as you don't propose to marry her, and as I don't propose to accept her services, the question isn't a particularly important one for either of us."

CHAPTER IV.

PERHAPS, it may be said, without offence to hospitable landowners, that the pleasures of staying in a large country house are somewhat dubious. Setting aside the uneasiness which most of us experience when deprived of our usual occupations and our accustomed play-things, and the misery of coming down to breakfast in the morning, cross and sleepy, to encounter a large assemblage of painfully wide-awake and smartly attired persons, one is seldom free from apprehensions as to the pro-gramme of the day's proceedings ; and, indeed, it only too often happens that one is either left to one's own devices—in which case one does not know what to do with oneself—or else expected to take part in some form of amusement for which one is peculiarly ill-fitted.

Possibly, however, these are only the ungracious murmurings of middle age. As there never seems to be any difficulty in filling big houses, it must be assumed that a great many people enjoy the kind of existence led there, and certainly Miss Sylvia Wentworth was enjoying herself to the full at Morecambe Priory. Although she passed for being something of a spoilt child, she did not, as a rule, enjoy herself very much at home. Her father did not put himself out of the way to provide diversions for her ; her tastes did not accord with Muriel's, and she saw a good deal less of life and the world than she could have wished. Consequently, it was no small treat to her to be taken under the wing of good-natured Lady Morecambe and to be allowed a glimpse of that section of society which, in some respects, resembles the lilies of the field and Solomon in all his glory. This little golden-haired, blue-eyed girl, whose prettiness was of that fragile order which cannot be expected to outlast many seasons, may have felt instinctively that it behoved her to make the most of her time. She fretted impatiently over the many wasted days which she was compelled to spend in London, deeming every day wasted that did not bring her entertainment in some shape or form, and resenting the selfishness of those who thus defrauded her of her youth. But at Morecambe Priory it was quite another affair; at Morecambe Priory there was a constant change of visitors, there were great ladies who amused themselves by petting her and men of all ages who delighted in paying her small attentions; so that it was really only an insignificant annoyance that Johnny Hill should have been invited to join the ranks of the latter.

She had dressed rather early for dinner one
evening, and was sitting in the library, awaiting
the appearance of the other guests, when
Johnny Hill shambled into the room and joined
her. He was a tall, loosely-built youth, with a
round, foolish face, not unlike his mother's; his
hands were large and red, and as he advanced,
she was struck by his underbred air. That
defect was not quite so conspicuous in London,
and indeed he was a good-natured creature with
whom she was willing enough to flirt in the
absence of higher game; but the fact was that
he was absurdly out of place amid his present
surroundings. Sylvia, it must be confessed, was
not wholly free from an outsider's ignoble
jealousy of other outsiders.

It was in a tone of mingled irritation and
patronage that she said :

" Well, Johnny, how do you like yourself
here ? "

After a moment of reflection, Mr. Hill replied in a deep, bass voice :

" I like being anywhere where you are."

" Thank you so very much ; I never met anybody who could pay a compliment with quite your grace and delicacy. But as we see each other so constantly in town, perhaps it would be only fair to other people if we were to avoid one another now that we are away for a change. You will be out shooting all day to-morrow, of course."

" Well, I don't know about all day," answered the young man, propping himself up against the mantelpiece and stuffing his hands into his pockets ; " I suppose we shall go out in the morning. Why do you say that we meet constantly in town ? It seems to me that you're always engaged when I try to see you."

" Then I can only suppose that you don't try

very hard or very frequently, for heaven knows that my engagements are not numerous!"

"I assure you," Mr. Hill declared with energy, "that of late I have been trying every blessed day."

"As often as that? Well, there's nothing like perseverance, and if you go on trying after I return home you are pretty safe to succeed in the long run. Just at present I'm not at home; I'm out for a holiday. Do you understand?"

The poor fellow's powers of comprehension were strictly limited, but he was scarcely dense enough to misunderstand that, although he could think of no appropriate rejoinder. He rubbed the back of his head feebly and remained silent until the entrance of Lady Morecambe, who was closely followed by several of her guests, relieved him of any further necessity for making himself agreeable. He dropped at once into the background, which seemed to be his natural place, and Sylvia would no doubt have forgotten his existence, had she not been unpleasantly reminded of it about ten minutes later, when he came forward to offer her his arm.

Happily, one always has two neighbours at dinner ; but, unhappily, one is not always acquainted with both of them, and Sylvia, on taking her place, deeply regretted that Lady Morecambe had omitted to introduce to her the gentleman who sat upon her right. She regretted it all the more because this newly-arrived guest looked a rather interesting sort of person. Although probably he was not a young man, his age was somewhat difficult to determine. His black hair and eyes and his well proportioned figure gave him a title to be called handsome, and he had the easy and slightly authoritative manner of one whose position is well established in society. She heard him

addressed several times as " Sir Harry," and observed that his remarks were listened to with a
deference for which their intrinsic worth seemed
scarcely sufficient to account. Apparently he
had been staying with various well - known
people, who had not had the good fortune to
succeed in amusing him ; for he had little to say
in praise of any of them, and complained that
everybody now-a-days was going in for political
meetings, which he stigmatised as the dullest
method of killing time that had ever been
invented.

Nothing is so likely to secure respect as a
heartfelt sense of superiority to those about
you, and this supercilious gentleman undoubtedly won his way to a higher place in
Sylvia Wentworth's esteem than he could have
done had he not been so obviously indifferent to
the fact that he had a pretty girl at his elbow.
After some considerable time, however, he

deigned to become aware of her presence, and, undeterred by the circumstance that he had not been formally presented to her, interrupted the conversation which poor Johnny Hill was labouring hard to keep alive.

"How do you contrive to amuse yourself here?" he inquired. "Do you hunt, or do you go out and watch the men shooting, or are you yourself a crack shot? I met a young lady the other day who could hit anything, including a beater. I saw her bag the beater, but she had presence of mind enough to swear that she was innocent, and I didn't tell upon her."

Sylvia replied that she, at any rate, could swear that she was innocent of any man's blood, never having fired off a gun in her life. She added that she thought it was easy enough for women to find amusements without attempting to take part in those which are usually supposed to be reserved for the other sex.

"Oh, I've no doubt you find it so," he returned, laughing; "and if you don't bring us down in one way you probably do in another. The only compensation that I have ever been able to discover for my advanced age is that I can now snap my fingers at you all."

"You call your age advanced because you want to be contradicted," Sylvia made so bold as to remark.

"Thanks for the compliment, but I scorn to deceive you. Besides, I am quite sure that if I tried to do so, you would look me up in the red book and put me to confusion. I shall be five-and-forty next birthday. Why I am neither grey nor bald I can't tell you, for I am sure I have had as much trouble as most people. I suppose it must be the immaculate purity of my conscience that has preserved me so well."

This was said in a voice loud enough to reach the ears of half-a-dozen persons, who did not laugh, but looked down at their plates with an air of grave abstraction. Thus Sylvia gathered that her interlocutor's conscience was not wholly void of offence, and thus, it must be owned, her interest in him was increased. In any case, he was better worth talking to than Johnny Hill, and the pains that she took to please him did not seem to be thrown away, inasmuch as he honoured her with his undivided attention until the time came for her to retire. He asked her a great many questions about herself and her belongings and pursuits, taking up a paternal sort of tone and deriving evident entertainment from some of her answers ; but he was not very communicative in return, and it was only after she had left the dining-room that she had the privilege of hearing a concise description of him from one of the dowagers.

"Oh, haven't you ever heard of Sir Harry Brewster?" the old lady said, in response to her queries. "He is a rather prominent personage upon the turf and—and elsewhere. Well, the less you see or hear of him the better, my dear, for he is not nice—not nice in any way."

Naturally that authoritative verdict did not prevent Sylvia Wentworth from thinking him nice, nor did it lessen her curiosity with regard to him. Later in the evening somebody proposed dancing in the saloon, which was a long room with a polished floor, easily cleared of superfluous furniture, and then it was that she found an opportunity of accosting her late neighbour, who had stationed himself in the doorway in the attitude of a spectator.

"Aren't you going to dance?" she asked.

"Oh no," he answered, shaking his head; "I leave that sort of thing to the young people."

"I am one of the young people," Miss Sylvia remarked demurely, "and I don't see much prospect of my getting a single respectable partner."

"In that case," he returned, laughing, "I will make so bold as to ask you for a dance. Heaven forbid that you should be deprived of respectability while I am here to represent it!"

Well, he was something more than respectable as a waltzer, whatever he might be in other ways; if he was wicked, he was not the less attractive on that account. A man whom old ladies speak of as "not nice" is usually understood by young ladies to be one who has made many conquests, and it is a part of feminine nature to adore conquerors of all kinds. Sir Harry Brewster did not give himself the airs of a conqueror, nor did he cease to treat Sylvia Wentworth as a child; but he confessed that he

6*

was flattered by her praise of his dancing, which emboldened him to monopolize her for the remainder of the evening. She enjoyed his company and conversation all the more because she caught Lady Morecambe glancing anxiously at her several times, and even because she saw Johnny Hill doing his best to look ferocious. To arouse the jealousy of Johnny Hill was a small triumph; but she did not despise small triumphs. As for her partner, she felt that it would be a great triumph to convert his somewhat condescending patronage of her into a warmer sentiment, and she unscrupulously made use of all the gifts which she had received from nature for the attainment of that end. However, she could not flatter herself that she had advanced far on the road towards success when she took leave of him.

"Good-night, Miss Wentworth," said he,

laughingly, "and thank you for having taken pity upon an old fogey. I suppose you know that I have been making myself ridiculous in the eyes of the youngsters all this time ; but never mind! I forgive you, and I daresay you won't do it again."

CHAPTER V.

LADY MORECAMBE was one of those well-intentioned, common-place persons to whom a wide experience of life is not of the slightest service and who never arrive at any clear comprehension of their fellow-mortals, because their memories are so short and because they never take the trouble to arrive at a clear comprehension of themselves. In her youth she had done many foolish things ; at middle age she was not wise, but she had learnt just as much as nobody can help learning, and she thought it incumbent upon her to speak a few cautionary words to the girl who had been placed for a time under her care. After breakfast, therefore, on the day following that of which some account has been given in the last chapter, she led Sylvia Went-worth away into the conservatory with her, and, while snipping off azaleas and dropping them into the basket which she carried, remarked casually :

" I was sorry to see that they had put you next to Sir Harry Brewster at dinner last night and that you danced with him in the even-ing. I purposely avoided introducing him to you."

" I thought him very pleasant," answered Sylvia. " What has he done that he can't be introduced to strangers ? "

" He has done all sorts of things which I am not going to tell you about. He is very bad indeed—shockingly bad. Indeed, I should never think of asking him here if Morecambe didn't insist upon it. You see, he happens to be one of the best shots in England, and when a

man enjoys that distinction he can't very well
be left out, whatever his moral character may
be. Only I can't be responsible for introducing
him to children like you, and I think it was very
bad form of him to speak to you without being
introduced."

"I was very glad that he did," Sylvia
declared. "He didn't contaminate me; he
talked to me like a father, and I was grateful to
him for delivering me from Johnny Hill. Please,
Lady Morecambe, don't send me in to dinner
with Johnny Hill again."

"I will try to find somebody else for you this
evening," her good-natured hostess answered;
"but I can promise you that it will not be Sir
Harry Brewster. You are much too young to
be told his history—you must take my word for
it that he is a dangerous acquaintance. All the
more so because he can be extremely fascinating
when he likes."

It would scarcely have been possible to be more injudicious. Sylvia made no rejoinder, but, of course, the warning only strengthened her determination to cultivate the acquaintance of the mysterious personage who neither looked nor talked like a reprobate. To doubt the sincerity of their own sex is a lesson which women learn at a very early age, and Sylvia was both unkind enough and precocious enough to suspect that Lady Morecambe's charms had failed to find favour in the sight of Sir Harry Brewster.

However, no immediate opportunity of bringing her personal charms to bear upon him was granted to her ; for all the men went out shooting in the morning, and, rather to her disappointment, no suggestion was made that the ladies should join them at the luncheon hour. It was not until late in the afternoon, when Lady Morecambe had gone off for a drive with

two venerable dowagers, that she was enabled
to join a party of the younger matrons who
proposed to walk towards the coverts and hear
the result of the day's sport.   This, it appeared,
had been quite magnificent.   She and her
companions had not tramped very far across
the wet grass when they encountered the
returning sportsmen, headed by Lord Morecambe, whose rosy countenance was radiant
with satisfaction.

"I can't think how the deuce he does it,"
Sylvia heard him saying, above the babble of
talk which immediately broke forth; "he simply
doesn't know how to miss!   And he has been
just the same for the last fifteen or twenty years,
mind you.   In all my born days I never saw
such a fellow!"

"He alludes to me," remarked somebody
who, as Sylvia very well knew, was standing
close behind her.   "Flattering, isn't it?   One

could have done without that allusion to the last twenty years, though. Ancient as I am, and well as I shoot, I will say for myself that I wasn't quite up to my present form before I attained my majority."

"Why do you always try to make yourself out so antiquated?" asked the girl, turning round and surveying Sir Harry's spare, erect figure. "A man is never old until he chooses to call himself so, and as for you, you couldn't be made to look anything but young."

Sir Harry laughed and bowed. "Thank you," he answered. "It is true that I look a year or two younger than I am, and that, I suppose, is what you mean; but there is no getting over the painful fact that I am old enough to be your father."

There are certain facts which have only such significance as we feel disposed to ascribe to them. Sylvia thought of her father, with his

scanty hair, his grey beard and his sedentary
habits, and laughed aloud. "You are a wonderful shot and a splendid dancer," said she, "perhaps you would neither be the one nor the other
if you were still a boy."

"If I could be a boy again, I would cheerfully consent to be unable to hit a haystack and
to dance like—who shall we say?—like your
young friend who took you in to dinner last
night. But as such bargains can't be made, the
only sensible plan is to make the most of the
privileges which belong to one's time of life.
While you are pounding round and round the
room at the county ball to-night I shall be
smoking a peaceful cigar before the fire, and
while you are poisoning yourselves with bad
champagne I shall be sleeping soundly, free
from all the troubles which I shall remember as
soon as I wake."

"One forgets one's troubles when one is

waltzing with a good partner," said Sylvia ; " I know that because I can speak from experience. Won't you come to the ball and try my prescription ? Even if it doesn't succeed in your case, you will have the comfort of thinking that you have done what you could to make it successful in mine."

" Am I to understand that you ask this as a personal favour ? " inquired Sir Harry, with a side glance which was half tender, half mocking.

Sylvia nodded.

" Well, then I must make an effort. Oh, yes ; I will certainly make an effort. Only if I fail at the last moment to come up to the scratch you will understand that exhausted nature or my natural diffidence or something of that sort has been too much for me."

Their colloquy was interrupted at this point, and they were allowed no subsequent chance of

resuming it. At dinner time, Lady Morecambe,
faithful to her undertaking, ordered a young
man who was not Johnny Hill to escort Sylvia,
and placed the whole length of the table
between her and Sir Harry Brewster. Immediately afterwards it was found necessary for
the ladies to go upstairs and put on their
ball dresses, and before Miss Sylvia Wentworth had studied the general effect of her
costume in the mirror half as long as she
could have desired, she received an impatient
message to the effect that everybody was waiting for her.

Everybody included Johnny Hill, and did not
include Sir Harry Brewster. She made that
unwelcome discovery after she had seated herself in the omnibus which was to convey her
and her fellow-revellers to the neighbouring
county town, Lady Morecambe, accompanied
by two of the more distinguished guests,

having already departed.   It appeared, however, that a relay of men was expected to
follow later on, so that there was still room
for hope.

Nevertheless, Miss Sylvia entered the ball·
room in an irritable mood.   Sir Harry Brewster
was nothing at all to her; still she had made
up her mind to dance with him, and she had
gone the length of begging him to be present at
this ball against his will, and she was neither
accustomed to being snubbed nor fond of the
sensation.

And so it was that, with some vague idea of
punishing the absentee, she filled up her card in
less than ten minutes.   That, of course, is what
a pretty, charmingly-dressed and well vouched-
for girl can accomplish without any difficulty if
she be not over particular, and Sylvia on this
occasion was not the least inclined to be particular.   Lady Morecambe, meaning to be kind,

led up to her a host of strangers, whose names she booked with the impartiality of total indifference; also she made Johnny Hill happy by granting him four dances all for himself. Having thus cut off her nose to spite her face, she began dancing, and kept an anxious eye fixed upon the doorway.

Now, as she was quite convinced that Sir Harry Brewster did not mean to keep his promise, it should have been no surprise to her to find him conspicuous by his absence from the knot of laggards who ultimately put in an appearance; but disappointments are seldom appreciated, and when a young lady who has not learnt the lesson of self-control is disappointed, somebody usually has to bear the brunt of her ill-humour. The luckless Johnny Hill took his punishment meekly. He did not resent being told, after a turn or two, that his step was simply impossible and that there was nothing for it but to sit out the remainder of the dance ; he submitted without a murmur to his partner's contemptuous disregard of the efforts that he made to entertain her, and he judged it best to agree with her when she declared that everything connected with this ball was detestable—the floor, the decorations, the music, the people, everything.

" I wish to goodness I had had the sense to stay at home ! " she exclaimed.

" I can't quite wish that," said this well-meaning young man. " Unless," he added, as a happy afterthought, " I had stayed at home with you."

" If I had stayed at home you wouldn't have been with me," returned Sylvia viciously. " If I had stayed at home I should have read a book and I should have been spared the labour of providing ideas for people who have none of their own."

This was rather unjust, considering that she had not as yet originated a single topic of conversation; but the provoking thing about Johnny was that injustice only bewildered him; it did not make him angry.

" I'm afraid," he said diffidently, after a pause, " that something has put you out."

Sylvia shot a wrathful, questioning glance at him; but perceiving that his countenance expressed only puzzled concern, she answered quickly :

" Nothing whatever has put me out, except the things that I have been telling you about, which ought to be sufficient, one would think. I wish they were sufficient to put me out in a literal sense; but I suppose it wouldn't be easy to get oneself ejected from a refined gathering like this. Nothing short of intoxication would do it, eh ? "

This being apparently a joke, Johnny felt

bound to laugh, although he felt some doubt
as to the good taste of the remark. But indeed
it was no longer of any consequence whether he
laughed or wept ; for his partner had suddenly
become totally oblivious of him. Whence Sir
Harry Brewster had sprung at that advanced
hour of the evening she was at a loss to
imagine ; but there he was, crossing the room
towards her with a smile upon his face, and it
was in the most matter-of-course tone in the
world he said :

"Well, Miss Wentworth, I have turned up to
claim my dance, you see."

Sylvia could not for the life of her help looking pleased ; but she contrived to reply with
befitting coldness and dignity, " Oh, you are
much too late ; my card was filled up ages ago."

And then, as he merely fell back, shrugging
his shoulders slightly and making a gesture of
resignation, she was fain to add, " You didn't

7*

expect me to keep anything open upon the off chance of your appearing in the small hours of the morning, did you ? "

"At the risk of appearing outrageously presumptuous," he replied, " I will confess that I did. You see, I shouldn't have been here at all if you hadn't ordered me to come. Of course I had no business to fall asleep after dinner ; but the moment that I woke I did all that mortal man could do to atone for my sin. What Morecambe will say when he hears that I drove one of his hunters over here in a dog-cart I can't think ; but I am assured that I risked my life by attempting such a thing ; so I hope you will admit that I have earned a dance even if I am not to be allowed one."

"Under the circumstances," said Sylvia, who felt that this explanation gave the offender a claim to be leniently dealt with, "I might throw somebody over." And without the

slightest compunction she turned to Johnny
Hill and told him that, after all, he couldn't
have number sixteen. " I promised it to Sir
Harry Brewster, only I thought he had forgotten."

Johnny, who was neither a well-bred nor a
reasonable being, had the audacity to protest.
He said that was really rather rough upon him.
He didn't see why he should give way to a man
who hadn't taken the trouble to be in the room
at the proper time, and he thought Sir Harry
Brewster might very well be content with an
extra.   There were sure to be some extras.
But Sylvia did not so much as pay him the
compliment of listening to his remonstrance.
Sir Harry offered her his arm and led her away,
while Johnny was left to reflect upon the extraordinary deficiency of all sense of honourable
obligation which seems to be characteristic of
the female sex.

If it would have comforted him in any measure to know that he was not the only person to whom Miss Sylvia proved faithless during the remainder of the evening, that melancholy consolation might have been his. She was, perhaps, too inexperienced to be aware that the throwing over of a partner means the acquisition of an implacable enemy, or too indifferent to trouble her head whether she made friends or enemies in a county which she did not inhabit. Either way, she danced with nobody but Sir Harry Brewster until the programme was exhausted, and, when her legitimate companions sought her out, dismissed them with a cynical coolness which at once flattered that gentleman's vanity and tickled his sense of humour.

"Do you make a habit of behaving in this way?" he asked. "It isn't for me to complain; but I doubt whether you would be wise to pay such a compliment to a man twenty, or even ten years younger."

"Oh, you needn't feel yourself compromised," she answered, laughing; "you know how to dance, and these people don't, that's all."

"That's all, is it? Well, I am glad I dance better than they do; but I should have been still more glad if you had preferred my company to theirs on other grounds. Are you still in the stage of regarding men merely as dancing-machines?"

"I have never been in that stage," Sylvia replied, "and I shouldn't think that anybody ever was. I only wanted to explain why I was thankful of any excuse to escape being bruised all over. Still, I daresay it won't make you very conceited if I own that I would rather talk to you than to a set of yokels. You at least have lived in the world."

He certainly had; and his acquaintance with

the world had imbued him with a poor opinion of its inhabitants. This, or a portion of it, he confided to the girl whose innocent blue eyes met his from time to time, and upon whom his moralisings were entirely thrown away. That story about the Dead Sea apples is a very stale one, and never since the world began has anybody's experience been of the slightest service to his neighbours. Yet, although Sylvia wanted to see the world, and meant to see it with her own eyes, she did not object to hearing its vanity exposed by one who knew it so well, and she did her best to draw rather more specific and personal statements from him. In that attempt she met with no great success ; but she arrived at the conclusion that he was not nearly as black as he was painted, and she was much pleased when he expressed a wish that they might meet again in London before long.

" I shall be going up for a week or two when

I leave this," he said. "Do you think Mr. Wentworth would allow me to call?"

"I am sure he would be very glad," answered Sylvia, "and so should I. You can't think what a dull life I lead at home. Muriel hates society. She goes to a certain number of dinners, to which I am not invited, and her one idea of amusing me seems to be to take me to a Saturday popular concert every week. That is all very well, but one doesn't meet people at Saturday populars, you know, except by some extraordinary chance."

"It won't be extraordinary if you meet me at one of them," returned Sir Harry, laughing, "because I shall make a point of attending them in future. I am rather fond of music, as it happens. Are you?"

Sylvia shook her head. "No; I think I rather hate it. I like doing things; I don't like sitting still and listening."

"I understand and I apologise. Let us begin to dance again forthwith."

But there was to be no more dancing for Sylvia that night; for before she could make any answer she was tapped on the shoulder by Lady Morecambe's fan, and Lady Morecambe's voice, which had an unwonted ring of asperity in it, said : "I am sorry to drag you away; but the carriage has been waiting nearly an hour, and perhaps it would look more dignified to retire now than to wait until we are God-save-the-Queened out of the place."

CHAPTER VI.

SYLVIA had only been invited to stay at Morecambe Priory until the day after the ball, but
she thought it extremely probable that she
would be asked to prolong her visit, and she had
every intention of yielding to persuasion. She
could not, therefore, manage to conceal her
disappointment when, on the following morning, Lady Morecambe intimated to her in a
cheerful, matter-of-course tone that a carriage
would be ready to take her to the station after
luncheon.

"I am very sorry my outing is at an end!"
she sighed.

"So are we all, my dear, I'm sure; but you

must come back to us. I will write and let you know when there are more entertainments in prospect and when we can get together a few people who will be likely to amuse you."

Sylvia declared that the present house-party was quite as amusing a one as she could wish for ; but Lady Morecambe was pleased to ignore that broad hint.

Without being a very strict chaperon, Lady Morecambe had no fancy for earning well-merited reproaches, and when a young girl who had been placed under her charge took to sitting out several consecutive dances with a man of Sir Harry Brewster's character, the time seemed to have arrived for packing that young girl off home as speedily as might be. Meanwhile, Sir Harry, who had breakfasted early, had gone out shooting, and there was no fear of his reappearance before dusk. His name was not mentioned to Sylvia ; but in the course of the morning she overheard Lady Morecambe speaking about him in an annoyed tone to one of the old ladies.

" I really don't see why a man should be allowed to take such liberties merely because he is rather more certain of hitting pheasants than other men. A horse that had never been in harness before ! If it had been anybody else, Morecambe would have been furious ; as it is, the unfortunate stud-groom has been blown up sky high."

The old lady here made some inaudible remarks ; to which Lady Morecambe re-plied : " Oh, of course I should take very good care to put a stop to anything of that kind."

It was easy to divine what was the kind of thing to which Lady Morecambe was so deter-mined to put a stop, and for the moment

Sylvia's sentiments with regard to her hostess were not those of gratitude or affection. How unkind and suspicious people were! What possible harm could she get from talking to a man who, as he himself had been careful to point out, was old enough to be her father? Anyhow, she would, if possible, say good-bye to him; and greatly vexed was she when it dawned upon her that this would not be possible. There were several men at luncheon; but the shooting-party was represented only by Johnny Hill, who explained that he had been " utterly off it, somehow or other," and had thought it best to come home.

The ill-advised Johnny followed her out of the dining-room into the library, whither she betook herself while waiting for the carriage to come round, and said reproachfully: " This is too bad of you! Why do you run away just when I have come down?"

" I give you my sacred word of honour," answered Sylvia, with emphasis, " that your presence or absence are not in the most remote way concerned with my movements."

" Oh, I know that," the young man returned quite humbly; " but it's a sell all the same. The ball last night was a sell too. If I was to be thrown over, I must say I would have been thrown over in favour of any man in the room rather than that fellow Brewster."

" I really don't see what difference it could make to you; but if you have anything unpleasant to say about Sir Harry Brewster, don't say it to me, please ; because I particularly like him."

" Oh, all right. You wouldn't like him so much if you knew a little more about him, though."

" I daresay I know as much about him as you

do: anyhow it doesn't interest me to listen to gossip. I quite understand your being jealous of him, because he shoots and dances so much better than you do ; but you ought to be prepared for meeting people of that description. There must be a good many of them in the world."

Having thus crushed her submissive admirer, Sylvia felt a little better and was able to take her leave without making it too apparent that she was conscious of having been sent away more or less in disgrace. But on the homeward journey her spirits gradually sank lower and lower ; so that she reached Upper Brook Street in a frame of mind which was far removed from amiability. To people of an irritable tempera-ment there is apt to be something provoking in returning, after a period of absence, to find everybody and everything exactly in their accustomed places—which must account for the somewhat unkindly greeting extended by Sylvia to her aunt.

"Oh, Muriel," she exclaimed, with a little vexed laugh, "why are you always having tea at half-past five?—and why are you always sitting in the same chair and looking as if you hadn't moved out of it for the last year or two? Do you *never* feel that you would like to make a change?"

Sylvia Wentworth had acquired a prescriptive right to behave like a spoilt child in the family circle. Her health was not good; some wiseacre of a doctor had said that she ought to be indulged, and the wiseacre's advice had been acted upon, with results which were scarcely satisfactory in the main.

Muriel only laughed and answered:

"I should like very much to make a change; but I doubt whether sitting in another chair or having tea a little earlier or later would answer the purpose.   Well, have you had a good time at Morecambe ? "

Sylvia unwound her boa, threw open her jacket and seated herself upon the hearthrug, holding up her hands to the blaze. " Pretty well," she replied. " The ball was rather a failure ; but there were some tolerably nice people staying in the house."

" Johnny Hill, amongst others, I hear."

" Oh, yes, Johnny was there. " *Why* he was there I can't imagine—poor wretch ! "

" Harriet Morecambe means to be good-natured," observed Muriel reflectively ; " I suppose somebody must have told her something.   But of course it is all perfect nonsense ; and I wish you would leave the unfortunate boy alone, Sylvia.   After all, he is hardly worth powder and shot, is he ? "

" Good gracious me ! you don't suppose I have expended powder and shot upon him, do you?" asked Sylvia disdainfully. "If ever I have insulted anybody in my life, I have insulted Johnny Hill; it isn't my fault if he doesn't mind, and it certainly wasn't my fault that he was asked to Morecambe. It wasn't my fault that I came away either; but Lady Morecambe wouldn't ask me to stay on. Oh, dear! what a deadly dull business life is! What have you been doing while I have been away? But I needn't ask. A few dinners, a few concerts and a little district visiting—the same old bill of fare day after day and week after week!"

Muriel did not care to mention such variety as had been introduced into it by the sermon and the visit of Mr. Compton, nor did Sylvia, when questioned as to the guests whom she had met at Morecambe Priory, care to mention the name of Sir Harry Brewster. Hence it will be inferred that no great sympathy existed between

8*

these two young ladies; although each of them was probably as sincerely attached to the other as to anybody else in the world. They seldom agreed; yet, by reason of the forbearance of the elder, they very seldom quarrelled; the only respect in which they could be said to be of one mind was that they were both thoroughly dissatisfied.

Therein they differed from Mr. Wentworth, whose epicurean philosophy led him to make the best of life as he found it, and who in fact found it quite tolerable. After a time he strolled into the drawing-room, kissed his daughter, said he hoped she had been enjoying herself, and, without waiting to hear her answer, asked Muriel who was coming to dinner next Thursday.

Muriel consulted a note-book and read out half-a-dozen names.

"You might chuck in the Hills mother and

son," said Mr. Wentworth. "Just now at the
club I came across that Colonel Medhurst whom
we met the other night, and I asked him. He
isn't a bad sort of fellow."

Muriel had no objection to Colonel Medhurst,
but demurred to the Hills. "Would they amalgamate very well with the others?" she asked
doubtfully.

"Oh, no, I shouldn't think they would; that's
one reason why I want them to come. Nothing
is more amusing than stirring up ingredients
which won't mix and watching the result.
Besides Mrs. Hill and I amalgamate splendidly;
I may say without undue vanity that if she is
placed next to me she will be happy. Perhaps
Sylvia will undertake the head of the Hill
family."

"That I most certainly will not," Sylvia declared resolutely. "Send me in to dinner with
any old bore you like; but at least spare me

Johnny Hill. Why, I have only just escaped from him !"

"Dear me !" said Mr. Wentworth, with a subdued chuckle; "I was quite under the impression that he was a friend of yours; since he isn't, far be it from me to inflict him upon you. No doubt your aunt can dispose otherwise of him. All I stipulate for is that the lovely and accomplished Mrs. Hill shall sit either on my right hand or my left."

It was easier to accede to his request than to Sylvia's; but, by some slight disregard of the strict rules of precedence, Muriel contrived to gratify them both, and if all the twelve persons who ranged themselves round Mr. Wentworth's dinner table on the following Thursday were not entirely contented with their neighbours, that, after all, is a misfortune of which hostesses often have to make the best. Mr. Wentworth was fond of giving small dinners, and took pleasure in incongruity, so that his sister had become inured to failures which he never would admit to be such. On this particular occasion she enjoyed herself individually rather more than usual; for Colonel Medhurst sat beside her and talked about Mr. Compton the whole time.

"Compton," said he, after eulogising his friend in no measured terms, "is one of the finest fellows living. All the same, if he were dead and if it were proposed to canonise him, I think I should know what to say as *advocatus diaboli.*"

"And what would that be?" Muriel inquired.

"It will be my duty to tell you when I hear of your having been admitted as a novice into the Society of S. Francis. For the present I will only say that he doesn't make enough allowance for human frailty. There are things which some of us *can't* do, and when a man keeps on asserting that we ought to do them he rouses the worst side of our nature into activity. But I daresay you will find that out for yourself later on."

Now, this was rather a clever sort of criticism for a simple-minded person like Colonel Medhurst to have made, and Muriel would gladly have pursued the subject further; but unluckily it was not uttered until the fag end of the dinner, so that she took a sense of unsatisfied curiosity upstairs with her. And then her thoughts were diverted from Colonel Medhurst and Mr. Compton by the strange behaviour of Sylvia, who declined in a most determined manner an invitation from Mrs. Hill which, judging by all precedent, she should have accepted with alacrity. Mrs. Hill was going to give what she called " an impromptu afternoon dance " on the following Saturday, and although there are, no doubt, many people who abhor afternoon dances, Sylvia Wentworth had never given her friends reason to suppose that she was one of them. Moreover, the excuse which she alleged was obviously insincere. In the first place, she had never promised to go to St. James's Hall with her aunt, and in the second place, if she had, she would have broken her promise without an instant's hesitation had she wished to do so.

However, Muriel was too considerate to raise her voice in protest. She remained neutral while her niece obstinately resisted the entreaties of Mrs. Hill and the grumblings of Johnny; and it was only after the party had broken up that she asked: "Why in the world are you so anxious to go to the next Saturday Popular, Sylvia?"

"Who told you that I was?" returned the girl. "I was anxious not to go to Mrs. Hill's,

that was all. You were preaching to me the
other day that I ought to leave Johnny Hill
alone, and the seed has fallen upon good ground.
I am resolved to let him alone, if he will only
allow me."

Well, it was permissible to doubt the absolute
honesty of that profession; but at any rate
Muriel could not suspect that a classical concert
possessed any special attraction for her niece.
It would have been as reasonable to surmise
that Beethoven's Symphony No. 4 in B-flat was
capable of attracting a sporting baronet. Yet—
for improbable events are always occurring—
St. James's Hall was graced, on Saturday afternoon, by the presence of the sporting baronet
and the unmusical young lady; and a very
provoking circumstance it was for one, if not for
both of them, that they were precluded from all
possibility of exchanging anything more than a
distant salute. What is the use of recognising a

friend from afar if you are placed in the very
middle of a row of stalls, with stolid and im-
movable persons all round you ? Sylvia frowned
and bit her lips and beat the devil's tattoo with
her little foot; but these manifestations of impotent wrath were wasted upon her neighbours,
who naturally did not understand that she
expected them to get up and walk about between
the pieces.

Nor was she any more fortunate when the
concert was over and the audience had begun to
disperse. That opportunity, it might have been
supposed, would be seized by any man in search
of opportunities ; it would have been so easy for
Sir Harry Brewster to shoulder his way through
the throng and offer to find Miss Wentworth's
carriage for her.

But it so chanced that Sir Harry's passage was
barred by two corpulent old women, and then,
as ill luck would have it, the footman, who was

seldom discoverable when wanted, was for once
on the alert ; so that poor Sylvia was hurried off
into the carriage before she had time to think of
dropping something and being obliged to return
for it.

"Oh, *hang* it all !" she scandalised Muriel by
exclaiming, as she threw herself back in her
corner.

Young ladies ought never to indulge in such
expressions ; but everyone will admit that a
coachman is entitled, under certain circumstances, to say something even stronger, and
Miss Wentworth's coachman made use of some
powerful and striking language when the near
horse caught his bit on the pole. The frightened
beast began to lash out ; the footman promptly
leapt down from the box, rather with a view
to insuring his personal safety than to render-
ing any assistance ; a crowd collected, and
a very pretty scrimmage ensued, in the midst

of which Muriel and Sylvia were dragged out
on to the pavement by some officious by-
standers.

Thus a chance was at length given to Sir
Harry Brewster, who, if he was too polite to
shoulder aside old ladies, had no such scruple
about scattering a street crowd. In a very short
space of time he had reached the horses' heads
and put matters straight; after which it became
his pleasing duty to reassure the two distressed
damsels.

"It is all right," he said, advancing towards
them, with his hat in his hand; "only I think
you will have to let me call a cab for you,
because you have broken a trace and your
splinter-bar has suffered."

And when Sylvia had introduced him to
her aunt and he had been thanked for his
timely aid, he improved the occasion by saying: "If you will excuse my telling you so,

you shouldn't use those old-fashioned bits, and you shouldn't drive about the streets of London without bearing-reins. You may depend upon it that you risk an accident every time you go out."

" I don't know about the bits," answered Sylvia, " but it was Muriel who insisted upon doing away with bearing-reins. She took it into her head that they were cruel."

Sir Harry explained that that was a mistake into which kind-hearted persons were very apt to fall ; bearing-reins were only cruel if you chose to make them so. He delivered a little lecture upon the subject while helping the ladies into their hansom, and there was a suggestion of expectancy about his demeanour when he wished them good-bye which moved Muriel to say hesitatingly that she hoped he would call in Upper Brook Street some day.

" I wonder whether it was the right thing to

do!" she murmured anxiously, after they had left him.

"Of course it was," answered Sylvia; "and I should have done it if you hadn't. I met him at Morecambe, you know. Isn't he nice?"

"He looks like a gentleman," observed Muriel guardedly.

"A gentleman? I should think so! Why he is—well, I can't tell you exactly what he is, but everybody knows him."

Under the circumstances, it was perhaps just as well for Miss Sylvia that her aunt was not everybody.

CHAPTER VII

MR. WENTWORTH pursed up his lips and raised his eyebrows when Muriel told him the name of the gentleman who had so obligingly befriended them.

"Sir Harry Brewster?" said he. "Well, you know—or rather perhaps you don't know, and after all, it's no business of ours. Only he hasn't had precisely an edifying career."

"I am very sorry I asked him to call," Muriel said; "but I didn't see how I could very well help it."

"Oh, that doesn't matter. His peculiarities are not likely to be infectious, and if he is good enough for Lady Morecambe, I suppose he is good enough for us. Still there is a certain quaintness in his having been taken up by you, of all people."

" I never thought of taking him up," answered Muriel, " I knew nothing whatever about him. But I do wish Lady Morecambe hadn't introduced him to Sylvia! All the more so because she has evidently conceived a great admiration for him."

" She is welcome to admire him as much as she likes," returned Mr. Wentworth placidly. " The man must be just about my own age."

" He doesn't look it," observed Muriel doubtfully.

" Thank you, my dear ; but if you will consult the recognised authorities, you will find that I am not very far wrong. He is by way of being completely ruined ; but that doesn't seem to interfere with his keeping a racing stable."

" I must try to be out when he calls," said Muriel in a meditative tone.

"I should think it is quite upon the cards that he will not force you to be so uncivil. At his time of life a man isn't usually so keen about making acquaintances out of his own set."

This was, no doubt, a perfectly just observation, and under ordinary circumstances it might have been as applicable to Sir Harry Brewster as to most of his contemporaries; but there were reasons which disposed Sir Harry to make an exception in favour of the Wentworth family. Sylvia had succeeded in fascinating him ; an easy feat to accomplish, many people might have said, but in reality not one within the capacities of every pretty little girl. He had not exactly fallen in love with her ; but he thought her charming, he was gratified, although he laughed at himself for being so, by the unconcealed preference with which she honoured him, and he felt that he would be doing himself a great unkindness if he were to lose sight of her.

Moreover, there was one other consideration which had presented itself to him in the light of a remote possibility. Mr. Wentworth had exaggerated in describing him as a ruined man ; but he had squandered fully three-fourths of a large fortune, and more than once of late he had had disagreeable experience of the inconveniences attendant upon lack of ready money. Well, Miss Wentworth, as he had understood, was an only child, and her father was said to be comfortably off—something might come of it. But indeed this notion was put forward chiefly by way of persuading his conscience (for he still possessed a conscience, somewhat the worse for wear and tear), that he was provided with what is generally held to be a sufficient excuse for following up a casual acquaintance with a young girl ; he did not seriously contemplate offering his hand to Miss Sylvia, nor could he suppose that her relations would hear of such an alliance.

9*

He was too old ; he was too poor ; above all, his record was too notoriously evil.   But as, after full consideration, he decided to call in Upper Brook Street, it will be perceived that the restraining influence of Sir Harry's conscience was not very powerful.

It so happened that on the afternoon which he selected for his visit a little group of ladies was assembled round Muriel's tea-table ; so that she was unable to keep watch and ward over him, as she would fain have done.   Diffidence not being amongst his failings, he was in no way chilled by the somewhat formal fashion in which she greeted him, but remained standing beside her for several minutes and talking with the assured ease and friendliness of one who does not doubt his welcome.   He then took up the cup of tea which she had poured out for him and calmly walked away with it to the sofa where Sylvia was seated.

" I have a crow to pluck with you," he began, as he placed himself beside her. " Why did you bolt away from Morecambe in that precipitate manner, without so much as allowing people a chance to bid you good-bye."

" I went away for the very good reason that my time was up," answered Sylvia. "One can't stay on in a house unless one is asked can one ? "

" Oh, I don't know. I always do, if I feel inclined. I don't very often feel inclined, though ; and certainly I didn't feel inclined to linger at Morecambe after your departure."

" Thank you very much," returned Sylvia with a low bow. " All the same, I don't believe you would have sacrificed a morning's shooting even if you had known that I was leaving."

" Oh, yes I should ; I should have sacrificed it quite cheerfully, at the risk of enraging Lady Morecambe, who thinks that every effort ought to be made to keep me out in the open air when I am staying with her. Lady Morecambe regards me as a reprobate, from whom it is necessary that the young and innocent should be warned off. I shouldn't wonder if she had told you so."

" A great many people are called reprobates," remarked Sylvia. " I don't know what it is that they are supposed to do or have done ; but I do know that they are much pleasanter to talk to than the saints or the dull respectabilities. Are you really so very much worse than your neighbours ? "

" I am afraid so ; but it is difficult to say, because one can't tell for certain how bad one's neighbours may be. Still I don't quite see why my past misdeeds should make me unfit to be spoken to. So far as our intercourse has gone, you have found me behave pretty well, haven't you ? "

" Oh, yes," answered Sylvia, laughing, " I have
no complaint to make."

She would have liked to hear something rather
more precise as to Sir Harry's alleged wicked-
ness; but the subject seemed to be one which
demanded delicate handling, and he did not
respond to her tentative allusions.   Doubtless he found it pleasanter and safer to
talk about her than about himself, and as
she had nothing to conceal, he was soon
made acquainted with all her aspirations and
grievances.

" It is so hateful to know that at the very best
one can only look forward to a few years of real
life!" she exclaimed ; "and to think that one
is throwing away day after day of the precious
time!   If a woman is clever, if she can *do*
something — such as writing or singing or
painting — or even if she is a sort of pious
enthusiast, like Muriel, it is different; but what

is to become of a helpless ignoramus after her youth is over?"

" I don't think I pity you so very much," said Sir Harry, smiling; "you have a good many years of youth before you yet. Besides, if you will allow a man of my age the privilege of impertinence, I will make so bold as to remind you that you possess one gift for which the clever women and the pious women would be glad to exchange all their talent and piety."

Sylvia did not think him impertinent; but she returned, somewhat petulantly, " I wish you wouldn't harp so upon your age! It makes me feel as if you thought me a silly child; and if I am to feel like that, I would rather not go on talking to you."

In the presence of that threat, Sir Harry promised amendment; and indeed she noticed that his tone had already become more friendly and less paternal than it had been at Morecambe

Priory. He did not talk like a lover, perhaps hardly even like a potential lover ; but he in- sinuated compliments, every now and then, which sounded pleasantly in her ears, and he propounded various schemes for her diversion. Did she think her father and her aunt would consent to make up a little party to the theatre some evening and allow him to entertain them at supper afterwards? Was she fond of coaching ? Because, if so, they might choose a fine day and drive down to Richmond or else- where.

" I have no coach of my own now-a-days," he added, with a laugh ; " times are too bad. But a friend of mine who has gone off to lose his money at Monte Carlo has left me in charge of his horses, and it is my duty to give them exercise."

All this was very delightful to Sylvia, who began to see blissful visions. Of course the

ambition to shine in the fashionable world is not
a very noble one; but ambitions are many and
nobility of purpose is rare.   Possibly there may
be personages holding exalted positions whose
moral level is not very much higher than was
that of Sylvia Wentworth.

The ladies who had been chattering over the
tea-table went away refreshed; others, to
Muriel's annoyance, came in and took their
places; but still Sir Harry lingered on.   As he
had truly said of himself, he always stayed when
he felt inclined to stay, and he might have added
that he always did what he was inclined to do:
he had known no other rule through life.   He
was at length about to rise and take his leave
when Mrs. Hill was shown into the room, followed
by the docile Johnny.

"Oh, *what* a nuisance!" groaned Sylvia;
"here are those dreadful people again!"

Sir Harry had an eye-glass, which he screwed

into his eye, surveying the new-comers. " Dear
me!" said he; " isn't that our young friend
whom you treated so abominably at the ball?
And that very ornate old lady is his Mamma, I
presume. Does she make a practice of leading
the poor fellow about in this way?"

"She does when she calls here," answered
Sylvia ruefully; " and the worst of it is that she
is for ever calling here. Whether Johnny likes
it or not I don't know; but he doesn't look as if
he did."

" I should imagine," said Sir Harry, with an
amused smile, " that he was not an unwilling
victim. What gives him that truculent expression just now is that he thinks I mean to
monopolise you all the time he is here. He
little knows how unselfish I am and how eager to
promote everybody's happiness."

Mrs. Hill came trotting across the room to
embrace her young friend. (If there was one

thing that Sylvia hated more than another, it was being kissed by Mrs. Hill, and she never failed to show her dislike of the salute after a fashion which there was no misunderstanding.)

" Well, my dear," the good-natured woman began, " I hope you enjoyed your concert the other day, though I can't help thinking that you would have enjoyed our little dance more. But I know you went to please Muriel, and that was very kind of you, and the next dance we give shall be in the evening, which I daresay you will like better. Johnny is very anxious to consult you about a cotillon. Do you think we could undertake such a thing with any prospect of success ? "

" Not if he led it," answered Sylvia gloomily.

Sir Harry Brewster was taking leave of Muriel, who was receiving his adieux with a dignified stateliness by which he did not seem to be in the least abashed.

" So sorry to have missed Mr. Wentworth,"
Sylvia heard him saying; "but I hope I may be
more fortunate another time."

Then he favoured Sylvia with a valedictory
smile, picked his way deftly through the obstruc-
tive pieces of furniture with which the drawing-
room was encumbered, and departed.

"What a fine-looking man!" Mrs. Hill exclaimed. "Who is he? Where did you meet
him? Would you like me to send him an invitation to our dance? Any friend of yours would
be most welcome, as I'm sure you know."

It fell to Muriel's lot to explain that Sir Harry
Brewster was not a friend, only a very slight acquaintance, and that she certainly did not know
him well enough to ask or accept invitations on
his behalf. Sylvia remained disdainfully silent.
Sir Harry, of course, would never dream of going
to Mrs. Hill's house, and it struck her as an
unwarrantable and provoking piece of presump-

tion on the latter's part even to suggest such a thing.

But a much greater act of presumption was about to be perpetrated by one who, whatever may have been his failings, did not often sin in that direction, and Sylvia's breath was fairly taken away when Johnny Hill, speaking in a subdued, but solemn and censorious voice, said :

" I was very sorry to see that man here; I hope you didn't ask him to call."

She was really too astonished to be angry. " My good boy," said she with calm contempt, " what do you know about Sir Harry Brewster ? And what business have you to be sorry or glad because he comes here ? "

" I am sorry because I can't help it," answered Johnny doggedly. " As for what I know about him, it isn't a secret—although you haven't been told, I suppose."

Sylvia's curiosity was too much for her dignity. Mrs. Hill was deeply engaged in conversation with Muriel ; Johnny had seated himself in front of her, with his elbows on his knees, and was looking anxiously into her face ; there was no fear that any communication which he might have to make would be overheard, and she did very much want to know of what mysterious crime Sir Harry Brewster had been guilty.

" Speak on," said she composedly ; "you have evidently got hold of some choice bit of scandal which will choke you unless you are allowed to utter it, and rather than see you drop off your chair in a fit, I will listen to you. Only it doesn't follow that I shall believe you, you know."

CHAPTER VIII.

"YOU may refuse to believe me," Johnny said ; " but you will be obliged to believe what I am going to tell you, because it can be so easily proved. It is just as well known as anything else that has been published in all the newspapers, and I can't understand why Lady Morecambe did not warn—speak to you, I mean, about it. Sir Harry Brewster was divorced from his wife two years ago."

Sylvia's colour changed ; but she laughed with a very fair show of indifference. "So that is the great mystery, is it?" said she. " Well, I don't see what concern his matrimonial misfortunes are of mine ; though of course I am sorry to hear that he didn't manage to hit it off with his wife.

It was all her fault, I daresay; it generally is the wife's fault in these cases."

Johnny was too meek to suggest that Miss Sylvia's knowledge of the causes which commonly bring husbands and wives into the Divorce court was probably limited ; he only replied, " It was not so in this case. There was not a word to be said against Lady Brewster, and Sir Harry scarcely attempted to defend himself. He only denied certain charges because—well, I can't go into it with you ; but there are certain charges which a man is supposed to deny. Whether they were true or not, quite enough was proved to make the poor woman sure of getting her divorce. It was a very bad case," added Johnny, shaking his head solemnly.

" How you enjoy saying that ! " exclaimed Sylvia irritably. " You couldn't look more sanctimonious or more—more idiotic if you were a newly-fledged curate ! "

Poor Johnny winced. He was very young; he naturally believed himself to be thoroughly acquainted with the world and its ways; it was not agreeable to him to be called sanctimonious, and it was even less agreeable to be likened to a curate.

" It *was* a very bad case," he repeated rather sullenly, "anybody whom you choose to ask will tell you so. As for me, I assure you I don't at all enjoy talking about such an unpleasant subject."

" Don't you?" returned Sylvia airily. " Then we won't talk about it any more."

At this unexpected rejoinder Johnny Hill gnawed his nails—a bad habit of which his mother had vainly endeavoured to cure him. " All right," he answered slowly; "only I hope you understand now that Sir Harry Brewster isn't the kind of man who has any business to be intimate here."

Sylvia pointed an admonishing forefinger at him. " If you mean to go on like this, Johnny," said she, " I shall certainly understand that you have no business to be intimate here. Do you really imagine that we shall allow you to revise our visiting list for us ? "

" Of course not ; only, you see, you hadn't heard about Sir Harry, and I daresay Miss Wentworth hasn't heard either. I'll just say a word to her before I go, and——"

Sylvia's small fingers gripped his arm with a force and suddenness which made him jump. " If you do," she interrupted, " I will never speak to you again ! Yes ; I mean it, I will never speak to you again—never ! Now, you needn't run away with the idea that I care a bit more for Sir Harry Brewster than I should for any other man who was nice and entertaining ; but it so happens that he is the only nice and entertaining man of my acquaintance, and I am

10*

not going to be deprived of him just because he
has a divorced wife somewhere or other. What
difference would it make to me if he had twenty
divorced wives ? "

" I can't help thinking that that kind of thing
does make a difference," said Johnny.

" It isn't a question of what you can't help
thinking ; the only person whose thoughts upon
the subject are of any consequence is papa.
You say everybody knows about Sir Harry ; so
I suppose he knows. Yet, you see, he doesn't
forbid him the house."

" Oh, if Mr. Wentworth approves of his coming here, there is no more to be said."

" Then don't say any more—at any rate not
to Muriel. She is so strait-laced that a word
or two would be enough to make her rush off to
papa, full of horror and dismay ; and then, for
the sake of peace and quietness, he would say,
' Oh, very well ; tell the servants not to let him

in again.' And if that misfortune were to happen through your fussy interference, I do most solemnly declare, Johnny, that I would never address another syllable to you for the rest of my days! You might talk and talk till you had no voice left, but I should remain as silent as the tomb."

Johnny ceased biting his nails, sighed heavily and said, " As you please."

It was, after all, true that Mr. Wentworth could not be ignorant of Sir Harry Brewster's history, and if Mr. Wentworth did not know that the man had been there that afternoon, he would certainly hear of it soon. It might also be true—Johnny tried to hope it was—that Sir Harry was attractive to Sylvia for no other reason than that he was entertaining. Finally, the girl was quite capable, if disobeyed, of carrying out her dreadful threat. So Johnny surrendered, and to reward him for his submission,

Sylvia not only bestowed a smile upon him, but, snatching a flower—any flower—out of the nearest vase, stuck it into his buttonhole for him.

" There ! " said she ; " that is because you are a good boy."

It was at this juncture that Mrs. Hill, who had been saying good-bye to Muriel for a matter of five minutes, turned round to beckon to her son ; and greatly pleased was she to see what an honour was bestowed upon him. Johnny was patient and dutiful ; yet there were moments when he felt that his mother was nothing short of a scourge, and his unerring instinct told him that one of these was now at hand.

"Oh, what a lovely flower ! " Mrs. Hill exclaimed. " Sylvia dear, how very kind of you ! But it is too bad to rob you !—and with flowers at such a price as they are now ! "

"I don't think this one could have cost a very large sum," answered Sylvia demurely ; "it's only a primula, and I'm sorry to see that it is a withered one into the bargain. Still," she added, turning to Johnny, with mock humility, "such as it is——"

The unhappy Johnny, conscious of being held up to ridicule, reddened, gobbled, and shaped a hasty course for the door, colliding heavily with a table on his way. His mother followed him, smiling all over and thoroughly satisfied with the success of her visit.

Muriel could not help joining in the burst of laughter to which Sylvia gave way as soon as the door had closed, though she felt bound to utter the usual remonstrance. "Why do you do such things? Why do you hurt the poor fellow's feelings in that way? What is the fun of it?"

"Can you sit there holding your sides, and ask me what is the fun of it?" returned Sylvia.

"All the same, I am innocent. I didn't want to hurt his feelings, and I'm sure I didn't expect to get any fun out of him. It was all that absurd old woman's doing."

"But what made you give him a flower?" persisted Muriel.

"I gave him a flower because I thought he deserved it," answered Sylvia oracularly; and perhaps it was because she did not wish to be questioned any further that she left the room.

Her face changed as soon as she was out upon the staircase, and by the time that she reached her bedroom all trace of merriment had vanished from it. She threw herself down in a capacious arm-chair by the fire-side (throughout the winter the fire was kept burning in Sylvia's bed-room), and, with her chin resting upon her hand, began to think over the disagreeable news that she had just heard. Being now alone, she admitted that it was disagreeable. She would not have minded hearing, in general terms, that Sir Harry Brewster had led a wild, dissipated, extravagant life; as much might be said of a great many heroes and fine fellows. But this, somehow, seemed to be a rather different affair. This implied—or at least she supposed it did— conduct quite the reverse of heroic. And yet, what right had she to condemn him without having heard both sides of the case? She resolved that she would find out the truth—if only she knew how to set about it! She could not condescend to catechise Johnny Hill; it would be rather a risk to question her father, and Lady Morecambe was out of reach.

"I know what I will do," she said at length, tapping with her little foot in a determined manner upon the hearthrug; "I will ask Sir Harry himself!"

At the same moment Muriel, downstairs in the drawing-room, was confiding some of her perplexities to Mr. Wentworth, who had just come in.

"Sir Harry Brewster called this afternoon and stayed a long time," she was saying. "He showed in the plainest possible way that he had come to see Sylvia; indeed, he scarcely spoke to anybody else. I didn't like it, and he saw that I didn't like it, and he was amused—which I must say I think was rather impertinent of him."

"I can find it in my heart to forgive him for that," observed Mr. Wentworth, tranquilly. "There is something about your way of demeaning yourself when you are annoyed, my dear, which is of a nature to overcome the gloom of the most saturnine temperaments. I couldn't exactly explain what it is; but I assure you it's irresistible. A mixture of frigid dignity and—"

"Oh, never mind!" interrupted Muriel; "it isn't my demeanour that signifies, but Sylvia's;

and I am sure she likes this man. I wish you would tell me what it is that is wrong about him."

" I'm afraid I can't. I am extremely modest, as you know, and the details of his career are scarcely fitted for the ears of a young person. However, I may mention that his wife divorced him—and showed all the requisite causes for so doing. *All* of them, you understand ? "

Muriel flushed indignantly. "That includes personal violence, doesn't it ? " she asked.

Mr. Wentworth nodded. " As far as I remember, she proved a box on the ear—and once, I think, he threw something at her. It may have been a chair, or it may have been only a newspaper ; anyhow, it was sufficient for her purpose."

" And quite sufficient," added Muriel, " to justify you in forbidding him ever to enter this house again."

"Oh, I don't know about that, he hasn't thrown anything at me yet, you see. I may be over-sensitive, but I confess that I shrink from making myself so supremely ridiculous as to suggest that I am afraid of my daughter's becoming enamoured of him."

"There would be nothing ridiculous at all in the suggestion," returned Muriel shortly. "It would be a great deal more ridiculous to expect that she will ever become enamoured of Johnny Hill."

"I must take the liberty of differing from you, my dear. Little girls don't fall in love with men who are well on the wrong side of forty, and Sir Harry Brewsters, when they marry a second time, espouse foolish widows with large fortunes. It isn't worth while to disregard all the known laws of human nature for the sake of providing yourself with an imaginary trouble."

So saying, Mr. Wentworth sauntered off to dress for dinner, leaving Muriel to knit her brows and sigh impatiently and wish she were less impotent. Impotent, however, she undoubtedly was, as she discovered later in the evening, when she took occasion to say to Sylvia : " I hope we shall see no more of that Sir Harry Brewster. It seems that he is divorced from his wife, whom he treated disgracefully. Your father has been telling me about it."

" Oh, I know that," answered Sylvia. " At least, I know he is divorced ; I don't know about the disgraceful treatment. Was papa angry at his having called ? "

And since truth compelled her aunt to confess that Mr. Wentworth had not been angry, she resumed : " Then I really don't care whether he is married or single or neither. I hope we shall see a great deal more of him. I think most likely we shall too."

This slightly defiant prediction was destined
to be fulfilled ; for a few days later came a note
from Sir Harry Brewster to say that he had
secured a box at the Lyceum theatre, which he
hoped that Mr. and Miss Wentworth and " Miss
Sylvia" would do him the honour to occupy,
and also that he had ordered supper to be in
readiness after the play, at a certain well-known
hotel.

It is by no means certain that Mr. Wentworth, who disliked turning out after dinner,
and who, in the matter of dramatic entertainments, infinitely preferred comic opera to
Shakespeare, would have accepted the above
invitation, had he not felt a malicious curiosity
to watch his sister's treatment of the hero of a
hundred scandals.   As it was, he decided to go ;
and against his decision there was no appeal.
He was amply indemnified for some sacrifice of
personal comfort by spending a very enjoyable

evening. Muriel, it is true, disappointed expectation, for she was simply cold, monosyllabic
and unapproachable ; but Sir Harry proved a
delightful companion.   He may have tried
to be agreeable to Mr. Wentworth ; but if so,
the effort was not apparent.   He was a good
talker ; he could tell a capital story without
taking too long about it ; above all, he was a
most appreciative listener.   With Sylvia his
manner was perfect.   He displayed just so
much admiration for her as a man of his
years is privileged to display ; there was a
touch of old-fashioned courtesy in his attentions to her ; he carefully abstained from
drawing her into anything like a private con·
versation, and if he did not altogether satisfy
the young lady, he at least convinced her father
that he was perfectly safe.

The supper, too, was above all praise. Mr.
Wentworth candidly avowed his amazement

that such cooking and such wine should be procurable in any London Hotel.

" But I'm an old fogey," he said ; " I can't pretend to have kept abreast of the times. I don't know how many years it is since I sat down to supper anywhere."

" My dear Mr. Wentworth," returned Sir Harry, " if you are an old fogey, it is only too plain that I must be another. However, your daughter is kind enough to say that I don't look like one, and I can honestly pass the compliment on to you. After all, I dare say we shall both of us be able to enjoy good things for some time to come yet."

It might, at all events, be safely predicted that neither of them would neglect any opportunity of so doing which might present itself ; and the circumstances being of a nature to promote a certain jollity and recklessness, there was no great difficulty about arranging that driving expedition upon which Sir Harry had set his heart. Muriel neither consented nor refused to join the proposed party. Conscious of being a wet blanket, yet unable to conceal feelings which there could be no possible use in displaying, she was almost as much displeased with herself as she was with her companions. For Sir Harry Brewster she had conceived a strong, and perhaps somewhat unreasonable antipathy.

Whether his attentions to Sylvia were seriously meant or not she could not tell; but it was beyond doubt that he was turning the girl's head, and it was extremely likely that he was preparing a great deal of unhappiness for her. Her brother's good-humoured selfishness filled her with indignation. No help was to be hoped for from him; and as for herself, what could she do? She was without authority and without influence.

" The only thing that makes me of the slightest value in the world," she reflected bitterly, " is my money ; and even money won't cure all evils. I wonder how large a bribe Sir Harry Brewster would ask to take himself off and never come back any more ! "

Now, Muriel Wentworth, if she had in some respects an ill-regulated mind, was no fool ; so she refrained from futile remonstrances and reached her bedroom that night without having put anybody in a rage. From the moment that her brother chose to make a friend of Sir Harry Brewster, there was nothing to be done, except to await the development of events and hope for the best. Some fine morning he would take fright — for he wished his daughter to marry well, and certainly, he could not wish her to lose her heart to a man who was out of the question as a husband—but until he realised the danger it would be vain to point it out to him.

Nevertheless, there was something very humiliating and very unsatisfactory in being so powerless.

On the following afternoon her thoughts were diverted into a rather more agreeable channel by a visit from Colonel Medhurst, who announced that he had come to ask whether she would care about inspecting " Compton's establishment." It appeared that Mrs. Sumner, the lady at whose house Muriel had made Colonel Medhurst's acquaintance, and who was more or less interested in the Society of S. Francis, had offered to escort him thither.

" And we thought," the ingenuous Colonel added, " that perhaps you might like to accompany us, if you haven't been there already. Have you any other engagement for Thursday afternoon ? "

No extraordinary powers of divination were required to conjecture that this proposition had

originated with Colonel Medhurst, not with
Mrs. Sumner; but in truth its cause was a
matter of complete indifference to Muriel, who
had more than one reason for welcoming it.

" Thursday would suit me very well, thank
you," she answered. " My brother and Sylvia
are going to drive down into the country with a
friend on that day, and I shall be glad of any
pretext for escaping the excursion. Besides, I
am very anxious to see Mr. Compton's establishment, as you call it."

" Ought it not to be called an establishment ?
It seems to be a brotherhood and a sisterhood
and a hospital and I don't know what else—all
under one roof. Anyhow, I also am anxious to
see it and prepared to admire it. Not that I
approve of Compton's principles, you know."

" So you gave me to understand. But perhaps
you haven't altogether grasped them yet."

" And you ? Well, we'll bring an impartial

criticism to bear upon him and all his works,
Miss Wentworth. He has promised to meet us
and act as showman, so that we shall have every
advantage."

This also was welcome news to Muriel. She
was not quite sure whether she wanted to snub
Mr. Compton or to consult him; but she was
quite sure that she wanted to see him again,
and her satisfaction shewed itself in the form
of gracious kindliness to her visitor, who went
away after a time, very well pleased with his
reception.

CHAPTER IX.

THE large red-brick building which was the
head-quarters of the Society of S. Francis stood
in a quiet little square within earshot of the
ceaseless traffic of Regent Street and Oxford
Street. It included within its walls, as Colonel
Medhurst had truly said, accommodation for the
male and female members of the confraternity,
as well as a hospital for children. It also con-
tained a richly - decorated chapel and a well-
stocked library ; so that the casual visitor might
reasonably infer—and usually did infer—that its
finances were in a flourishing condition. As a
matter of fact, however, the Society, like all
charitable societies which have any vitality in

them, found its funds inadequate to the demands made upon them ; and that was one reason why Mr. Compton, despite his multifarious occupations, felt bound to welcome casual visitors. Any hasty and erroneous impressions which they might have formed could be corrected by an inspection of his accounts, and after the existence of a deficit had been made clear to them they could hardly go away without leaving some pecuniary memento behind them.

" That is the worst of going to see Mr. Compton," remarked Mrs. Sumner to Muriel, who was sitting beside her in her open carriage, Colonel Medhurst facing them, with his back to the horses ; "one really isn't rich enough to do it often. It's almost as bad as going to the Home for Lost Dogs. One can't buy all the poor dogs and one can't provide for all the sick children ; so that one would consult one's own comfort by remaining away. However, you will both of you be immensely interested, I know; and if you empty your purses you will empty them in a good cause."

Colonel Medhurst examined the contents of his waistcoat pocket. "Two pounds three and sixpence," said he meditatively. "Compton will have to be satisfied with thirty shillings, because I must reserve myself a little change to play pool with at the club, after you ladies have dismissed me."

"Is that the way in which you generally employ your spare time?" asked Muriel, with a touch of scorn.

"I should feel truly grateful if you could tell me of a better," answered the Colonel, good-humouredly; "but I assure you it is no such easy matter for a soldier on leave to find occupations for himself in London. I haven't many friends, and I can't afford to train down to the country and hunt. Now I wonder what you would do, Miss Wentworth, if you were in my place."

But, as it was not Muriel's business to imagine herself in Colonel Medhurst's place or to devise employment for him, she only shrugged her shoulders. She was, after all, very much in his predicament, without his excuse, and perhaps it is quite as unprofitable to doze over afternoon tea as to play billiards at a club. Mr. Compton, to be sure, had hinted that he could find work for her; but he had been so uncomplimentary, and had shown so plainly that he did not care about being bothered with her, that she hesitated to remind him of that half promise. She was, in truth, by no means disinclined to quarrel with the man to whose direction she had been willing to submit her fortune and her future; one does not make such offers as that with the expectation of being benevolently smiled at.

However, when the carriage stopped before

the iron gates, surmounted by a cross, which gave admittance to the Franciscan edifice, and when Mr. Compton, attired in a black cassock with a cord knotted round his waist, came down to the steps to receive his visitors, it was evident that no immediate occasion for quarrelling with him was likely to present itself. He shook hands with them all ; he was very polite and pleasant, and if there was something in his manner which suggested the idea that he might be rather in a hurry, he made no verbal admission to that effect.

" I am quite at your service," he cut short Mrs. Sumner's apologies by saying, " and the children, as you know, are always delighted to see you. I must thank you in their name for the toys that you so kindly sent. But before we go to their part of the house, I dare say Miss Wentworth would like to have a look at our quarters and at the chapel."

The corridor through which he led the way with Mrs. Sumner was a narrow one, so that Muriel and Colonel Medhurst perforce brought up the rear. At the entrance of the chapel Compton removed his biretta and made a genu-flexion to the altar ; whereupon Mrs. Sumner, who always endeavoured to do the right thing, went through that somewhat ungraceful form of obeisance which is commonly known as a " Royalty bob." Muriel did not imitate her, but gazed up the dark aisle, over which there hovered a faint smell of incense, and sighed wistfully. How happy, she thought, must the men and women be who, after toiling all the day in the outer world, could withdraw to such a peaceful, silent and beautiful place of worship as this !

The chapel was a really good specimen of the modern variety of Gothic architecture. It was very ornate ; but the effect of the variously

tinted marbles, the stained glass and the
mosaics was not inharmonious, and the rich-
ness of the colouring was subdued by the dim
light. Compton pointed out some frescoes, the
work of a celebrated artist and the gift of one
of his wealthy patronesses ; he also drew attention to a few well-executed brasses which had
been presented as memorials. No guide could
have been more courteous ; but both in the
chapel and in the library, whither they presently
repaired, Muriel, watching him, was impressed
with the conviction that the sooner his task was
discharged the better he would be pleased.

Two smooth-shaven young clergymen, dressed
in the same costume as their chief, were writing
at the broad table which ran down the centre of
the library. They rose as the strangers entered,
were duly introduced and uttered a few commonplaces. One of them apparently asked for some
instructions from Mr. Compton, which were

delivered to him in a rapid, authoritative under-
tone.

"Our friend is a bit of a martinet, I suspect,"
whispered Colonel Medhurst to Muriel, "and
quite right too. I know by experience that you
can't command even a well-disciplined regiment
without asserting your personal authority pretty
firmly, and I can imagine what it must be to
keep a herd of excitable devotees, male and
female, under control. He seems to do it,
though."

Whether he did it or not, he certainly seemed
to be invested with despotic powers. All the time
that he was exhibiting the arrangements of the
institution—the refectory, the waiting-rooms, the
scantily-furnished bedrooms set apart for the use
of such members of the staff as were working in
London—he was being continually interrupted
by messengers who came to ask for orders or to
hand him papers which required his signature.

All this he took as a matter of course. It did not worry him ; but it discouraged Muriel, who began to perceive that there was little hope of her obtaining so much as five minutes of private conversation with so busy a man.

Possibly, however, he wished to speak a few words to her, or guessed that she wished to speak to him ; for when he had led the way into a bright airy ward where some twenty or thirty children were lying in their cots, he fell back and joined her.

"Now, Medhurst," said he, "I will leave Mrs. Sumner to introduce you to her little friends. My nose is quite put out of joint when I bring her here, because her advent is always preceded by a shower of toys."

Colonel Medhurst smilingly obeyed what was not so much a hint as a command ; and then this peremptory little priest began, without any preliminaries :

" Well, are you still in the same mind ? "

Muriel's face lightened up with pleased surprise. "Certainly I am," she answered. " And
have you changed yours ? Are you willing to
admit me ? "

"Oh dear, no! I told you there could be no
immediate question of that—probably no ultimate question. I was only wondering whether
I had completely choked you off by what I know
you considered my ingratitude."

" I never thought you ungrateful ; I asked a
favour, I didn't confer one. But I did think,
and I think still, that the reasons which you
gave were insufficient. You yourself would
think so if you realised what my position is
and what sort of life I lead. I am utterly use-
less at home ; my brother wouldn't miss me, and
I am supposed to be too young or too weak-
minded or something to be of any service to my
niece. I can only stand and look on at things

which—well, there is no time to explain; but sometimes I feel it almost unbearable."

He nodded. "Yes, I know; I have made some inquiries and I understand how you are situated rather better than I did. Still I couldn't advise you to desert your post even if it were as unsatisfactory as you make out— which it isn't. Are you fond of children?"

"Yes; I think I get on better with them, as a rule, than with adults."

"Then you might sometimes come here and help to amuse these waifs and strays. Those whom you see are the best cases, though some of them are incurable, I am afraid. We have another ward which we think it best to leave entirely under the charge of the Sisters; but here visitors are always welcome and are always a help to us. If you will look in occasionally it will fill up your spare time and may do something towards clearing your mind of morbid ideas. I can conscientiously assure you that you will be of use by coming."

"Thank you," answered Muriel; "I will come. But is that to be all?"

"That is all that I can do for you at present. You imagine that you have a vocation. You may be right or you may be wrong—most likely you are wrong. But in any case you can't expect us to accept your mere assertion ; it is for you to give us proofs, and convincing proofs. Do you understand?"

It was not a very encouraging, perhaps not a very polite speech ; but Muriel fancied that there was a slightly more sympathising look in the speaker's eyes than she had been able to discern there during their first interview. Besides, she was less exacting now than she had been then.

"I understand," she answered, "that you insist upon my starting from the lowest step of the

ladder.   I suppose I have no right to complain ;
but—do you take these excessive precautions in
every case ? "

" Not in cases where they would be excessive.
Now Mrs. Sumner has made her round, I see,
and is anxious to be released.   I will give
instructions that you are always to be admitted
when you come here.   One of the Sisters will
receive you."

It was evident that he was quite as anxious to
be released as Mrs. Sumner could be.   He conducted the party downstairs, accepted Colonel
Medhurst's dole with thanks and took his leave
n the space of a very few minutes.

" Isn't he quite wonderful ? " Mrs. Sumner
exclaimed, as she stepped into her carriage.
" So full of energy, and so simple and unaffected
with it all !   Of course one can't help regretting
his extreme notions, and it seems a great pity
that Lord Chepstow should have quarrelled with

him; still if he were not so unlike the rest of the world, I daresay he wouldn't be so interesting. Shall I take you straight home, Muriel? I have some visits to pay; but we will go to Brook Street first, if you like."

Muriel said she wanted a little exercise, and would prefer to walk home ; whereupon Colonel Medhurst promptly offered to escort her. He looked incredulous when he was assured that young ladies required no escort in the streets of London now-a-days; it had not been so previous to his departure for India, he said. Moreover, setting other considerations aside, how was she to get across Regent Street without somebody to take care that she was not run over by an omnibus? If Muriel had objected to his company, his representations would doubtless have proved ineffectual ; but she did not object to it. It was very much the same thing to her whether she walked home with Colonel Medhurst or alone ; perhaps, if anything, she had a slight preference in favour of the society of an old friend of Mr. Compton's.

However, Mr. Compton's old friend was disposed to be critical rather than laudatory. "Good works are good works," said he, "and I am glad to see the children made comfortable and happy, poor little souls, and—and Compton is a stirring orator. But the whole thing seems to be intended as a means towards an end, and I can't quite gather what that end is. Compton takes a good deal of trouble to keep it in the background."

"I suppose," answered Muriel, "that he doesn't see the use of talking about it to people who would neither agree with him nor understand him ; but I believe he makes no secret of his revolutionary opinions. He thinks the so-called Christian nations are living like heathens —and so do I."

" Will you make them less like heathens by
taking the veil, Miss Wentworth ? "

" I should make one unit among them less
like a heathen by joining the Society of S.
Francis, which is a very different thing from
taking the veil ; but I am not likely to join the
Society, because Mr. Compton is not likely to
admit me."

" He would deserve hanging if he did ! "
returned Medhurst warmly, and added, after a
pause, " It isn't natural, you know, Miss Wentworth."

" What isn't natural ? " Muriel enquired.

" Your wishing to withdraw from the world at
your age. I can't believe that you really wish
it."

" Nor can Mr. Compton. In other words, you
can neither of you give me credit for anything
but selfish motives. Well, perhaps you are
right ; perhaps I shouldn't want to leave the

little world in which I live if I could make it
move in the way that I should like. Yet I really
don't think I am a selfish person in the ordinary
acceptation of the term."

" I am quite sure you are not," Medhurst
declared confidently.

" Oh, you can't know anything about it. What
I mean is that I believe I should be happy
enough if I could make the people whom I care
for happy. Unluckily they think that they are
better judges than I of what may be expected to
bring them happiness."

What Muriel stood most in need of at this
moment, was no doubt, a sensible and sympathising confidant, and it may have been for
that reason that she was led to impart some of
her domestic sorrows to Colonel Medhurst, who
listened to her with kindly interest. She mentioned no names ; but he gathered that her niece
was in some danger of marrying a very undesir-

able person, that she was powerless to avert the calamity, and that Mr. Wentworth was too supine to take the precautions which a father ought to take.   He was very discreet in his replies.   He did not presume to offer advice and contented himself with commonplace consolations ; only he managed to convey to his hearer the impression that he would be only too glad to serve her by any means that might be within his power—which would have been adroit of him, had he harboured a deep design for winning his way into her good graces.   When she shook hands with him at parting her spirits had risen by a good many degrees ; for she felt that she had gained a friend.

But Medhurst, examining himself seriously that evening, was not sure that he could be satisfied with being only Miss Wentworth's friend.   Before he went to bed he stood for a long time before the looking-glass, studying his

face, which struck him as being deplorably
lined, weather-beaten and unattractive.

" Well," he exclaimed at last, "you *are* an old
fool ! "

And neither his glass nor his common-sense
had anything to urge in contradiction of that
uncivil criticism.

CHAPTER X.

To go straight to head-quarters for information sounds like a wise principle to act upon ; and indeed the system is said to have been adopted with success by certain eminent statesmen and diplomatists. Yet, if the truth were known, it might possibly be found that the statesmen have not wholly disdained other means of arriving at their ends ; because, unfortunately, the desire of the candid inquirer for a plain statement of facts is not always shared at head-quarters. No one, therefore, will be surprised to hear that Sylvia, in spite of her bold resolution to interrogate Sir Harry Brewster as to the circumstances connected with his divorce, knew very little more about them at the end of three weeks than she had done at the beginning. She did, indeed, summon up courage to put a point-blank question to him ; but his reply was such as to render further questions almost impossible. It was too true he said that he was a divorced man ; but Miss Sylvia would understand that he could not talk much to her upon such a subject. He might add that it was an excessively painful one to him.

After that, what more could she do ? She ventured upon an occasional hint ; but these he ignored, and finally she said to herself that she really did not care to pry into matters which were none of her business. The past was past and had better be forgotten : the present was quite enjoyable enough to content her.

If the present had not contented her, no blame could have attached to Sir Harry Brewster, who was indefatigable in devising schemes for her amusement.

Although he did not come very often to the house, he contrived to make arrangements for meeting Sylvia almost every day of the week, and what was still more clever of him was that he also contrived to secure the necessary escort in the person of her father. Mr. Wentworth did not mind incurring a little trouble and inconvenience for the pleasure of Sir Harry's society. Sir Harry was not only himself entertaining, but had a number of entertaining friends whom it was a change and an amusement to meet. As for Muriel's apprehensions and warnings, they were preposterous upon the face of them ; impossibilities do not occur, and Mr. Wentworth had a comfortable habit of treating all disagreeable occurrences as impossible.

Muriel herself ended by shutting her eyes to what, after all, was not obtruded upon her notice.

When one is helpless, one may as well hope for
the best : moreover, she had now a good deal
more to occupy her thoughts than she had
hitherto had.   Every day she spent several
hours with the sick children, whose affections
she had no difficulty in gaining: the sisters
made her welcome and were not averse to
chatting with her about the rules of the Society
to which they belonged and in the principles of
which they had the firmest faith ; from time to
time she encountered Mr. Compton, who was
always in a hurry, yet never passed her without
saying a few friendly words, and she had come
to look forward to the visits of Colonel Medhurst,
who frequently happened to drop in about tea-
time.   Upon the whole, her life just now was
pleasant to her, notwithstanding the modesty of
its immediate aims ; and, that being so, she was
disposed to take a more sanguine view of the
proceedings and prospects of others.

One day Sylvia received a letter which ought to have delighted her, yet, somehow or other, failed to produce that effect, and the contents of which she did not at once communicate to Muriel.

" We are going to have our annual ball next Wednesday," Lady Morecambe wrote, " and there will be two others in the neighbourhood in the course of the week ; so you see the time has come for you to redeem your promise. We shall expect you on Monday, and I will undertake to provide you with as many good partners as you can wish for."

Instead of jumping for joy, Sylvia found herself wondering whether she could not find some excuse for declining this seductive invitation, and it must be acknowledged that at first she was a little surprised by her own hesitation. However, she accounted for it by reflecting that she really had not more than one ball-dress fit to wear and

that she could not afford two new ones ; also
that balls were poor fun when you hadn't an
idea of who your partners would be ; finally
that Sir Harry Brewster had promised to take
her to see a polo match on the day named
by Lady Morecambe. The approach of the
post hour found her still irresolute, and she
was sitting at her aunt's writing-table in the
drawing-room, biting the end of her pen
and sighing, when Sir Harry Brewster was
announced.

Sir Harry, who was always careful to observe
the laws of conventionality, hastened to explain
that he had asked for Miss Wentworth and had
been told that she was at home.

"One Miss Wentworth is at home," answered
Sylvia laughing, " and the other will be soon.
Sit down and help me invent a polite fib.
Lady Morecambe has asked me to go down
to them next Monday for their ball, and I

don't think I want to go. What shall I say
to her ? "

" When I don't want to accept an invitation,"
observed Sir Harry, " I always say I am afraid I
can't manage it ; but perhaps ladies are expected
to give reasons. Why don't you want to go,
though ? It's sure to be well done, and I expect
you would enjoy it." He added presently, " I'll
go, if you will."

" Have you been invited ? " asked Sylvia, with
a sudden change of countenance.

" No ; but that's a trifle. I'll get Morecambe
to ask me."

Sylvia looked down and began to draw
patterns upon the sheet of paper before her.
" Do you know," she said hesitatingly at length,
" I don't think Lady Morecambe quite—likes
you."

" Oh, if that's all, I'm sure she doesn't," he
replied. " Lady Morecambe is—shall we say

prejudiced against me ? " Then, perceiving what
he was probably meant to understand, he resumed : " I shan't beg for my invitation until the
last moment, you know, and I shan't apply to
her ladyship at all. Meanwhile, please write an
acceptance. I'll undertake to say that when you
enter the ball-room you will find me on the spot,
waiting to claim a dance."

From the above fragment of dialogue it will be
seen that three weeks had brought about a
decided change of relations between these two
persons, and that Sir Harry had, consciously or
unconsciously, ceased to pose as the benevolent
admirer of mature years. Sylvia scribbled off
the letter, pausing every now and again to throw
a remark over her shoulder.

" I don't know why Lady Morecambe should
be prejudiced against you," was one of these.

" Oh, I think you do," responded Sir Harry
tranquilly. " In a general way of speaking, the

British matron is prejudiced against me, and the British matron is not wrong. I don't complain —but at the same time I must confess that I don't care. So long as you don't share the good lady's prejudices, she is very welcome to them."

" But perhaps I should," observed Sylvia turning a somewhat uneasy countenance towards him, " if ——"

" If you were as well acquainted with my misdeeds as she is? Very likely you would ; and that is why I shall not confess them to you. I will only take the liberty of pleading that I am not quite so black as I am painted."

During the period of silence which followed this audacious assertion Muriel came in and recognised the visitor with a look of annoyed surprise which did not escape his notice.

" You will have to dismiss your butler, Miss Wentworth," said he ; " his mind is too logical for his position. You have evidently given him

a general order to the effect that you are always
out when you are at home, and a deductive
process of reasoning has led him to conclude that
you must be at home when you are out. Anyhow, he assured me that you were at home, and
on the faith of that statement I followed him
upstairs. I can't pretend that I regret having
done so—especially as I arrived just in time to
persuade Miss Sylvia that she ought to accept
an invitation to Lady Morecambe's ball which
she was thinking of refusing. Nobody under-
stands how to make a country ball go off better
than Lady Morecambe."

" I had not heard anything about it; Sylvia
did not mention it to me," said Muriel, with a
perplexed look. And then, as her niece vouch-
safed no remark: " Are *you* going to this ball,
Sir Harry ? " she inquired.

" I am sorry to say that I haven't been asked,"
replied Sir Harry imperturbably.

Sylvia bent over the envelope which she was addressing. She was perhaps a little ashamed of her confederate's *suppressio veri ;* but on the other hand, the fact that he was making himself her confederate was not disagreeable to her. As for Muriel, she both felt relieved and looked so.

"Of course you will go, Sylvia," she said. "When did you ever refuse an invitation to a ball ? "

"Oh, I am going," answered Sylvia. "Only I doubted about it because Lady Morecambe says there are to be two other dances, and I have neither frocks nor money to buy them."

"If that is all, I'll provide the frocks," said Muriel, who indeed was in the habit of supplementing her niece's allowance by frequent gifts of that description.

In the innocence of her heart, she felt quite grateful to Sir Harry for having urged this change of scene upon Sylvia, and began to think

13*

that, bad as he was, she might have wronged him by suspecting him of designs which only a hardened scoundrel could have entertained. It was, therefore, with unwonted graciousness that she said : " I hope you will stay and have a cup of tea with us."

" He will be delighted," answered Sylvia for him. "I say so to save him from telling a direct falsehood. Sir Harry would prefer a sherry and bitters ; he doesn't really like tea ; no *man* does. Not even your long, solemn soldier, Muriel, though he meekly swallows about a quart of it every afternoon to please you."

Muriel, slightly displeased, was beginning to say that neither Sir Harry Brewster nor anyone else gave her the least pleasure by swallowing what he did not like, when she was interrupted by the entrance of the long solemn soldier, whose arrival at that hour had, to tell the truth, become a matter of almost daily occurrence.

The candles had not yet been lighted; so that Colonel Medhurst did not notice the presence of a stranger until after he had exchanged a few remarks with Muriel and had turned to shake hands with Sylvia. The latter, since her aunt said nothing, took upon herself to accomplish an introduction by which both men appeared to be disagreeably affected. Sir Harry, on hearing the name of Colonel Medhurst, rose hastily, made a half bow and looked round for his hat, while the other, standing stock-still, clenched his fists and muttered something suspiciously like an imprecation. There was a brief pause; after which the Colonel, whose voice was trembling with anger, said:

"I have not tried to meet you, Sir Harry Brewster; I know that I should gain nothing, except a little personal satisfaction, from giving you the thrashing that you so richly deserve. But since chance has brought us together in this very unexpected way, I will take this opportunity of telling you that you are no gentleman and that you have no business to be in any lady's house. I am sure if Miss Wentworth knew as much about you as I know, she would not permit you to enter hers."

"My good man," returned Sir Harry calmly, "there is one thing which certainly ought not to take place in any lady's house, and that is a brawl. Here is my card. If you wish to thrash me and think you can do it, by all means call upon me at any hour which it may please you to appoint ; but, for your own sake, don't indulge in strong language under circumstances which make it impossible for me to answer you."

Colonel Medhurst was one of those quiet, sensible men who very seldom lose their temper, and who consequently have had little practice in the difficult task of self-control.

"I am not going to treat you as if you were

a gentleman," he retorted, forgetting that he was asked to show some consideration for his hostess, not for his enemy. " Wherever I meet you I shall say what I said just now, and, as you very well know, I can justify my words."

" In that case," observed Sir Harry, "it is evident that one or other of us must retire. I will leave you to explain and excuse your behaviour to Miss Wentworth. No doubt, if she thinks it worth while, she will allow me to state my own case some other time."

He then took his leave in a manner which was not devoid of quiet dignity; and, as the slight pressure which he ventured to give to Sylvia's fingers was distinctly returned, he went away without much fear as to ultimate results.

Yet his predicament was really an awkward one, as he might have realised, had he not been rendered a little dull of comprehension by the comparative facility with which he had regained his position in society, after a temporary period of eclipse. Medhurst, when he was left alone with the ladies, grew a little cooler, though he was still much agitated.

" I suppose I ought to make you an apology," he began ; " I ought not, perhaps, to have brought about a scene in your drawing-room. But I think you will forgive me when I tell you that that man was my sister's husband and that she was compelled to obtain a divorce from him while I was away in India. You won't wish or expect me to give you all the particulars of the case ; but I may say this—that she proved personal cruelty. He struck her on more than one occasion before the servants. And the worst of it is that he has not been punished ; he was glad to be set free. It is she, and she alone, who has suffered."

" I don't think you owe us any apology,

Colonel Medhurst," said Muriel, who looked penitent and ashamed. " I knew—my brother told me—about the divorce ; but I didn't know who Sir Harry's wife had been."

" Your brother told you, and yet you continued to receive him ! " exclaimed Medhurst. " Well—I am surprised. I must say that I am surprised."

Muriel, feeling that it would be a little undignified to plead her own repeatedly expressed reluctance to receive the culprit, remained silent ; but Sylvia said :

" Why are we to condemn Sir Harry unheard ? Of course you are angry and you won't admit that there can be anything to be said for him ; but there *are* always two sides to a case."

" It is impossible to explain away facts which have been proved in a court of law," returned Colonel Medhurst coldly. " If you will excuse me, I will say good night now. I am sorry that this encounter should not have taken place else-where; but as regards what I said to that man I have nothing to retract and nothing to regret."

" I can't compliment your friend upon his manners," remarked Sylvia, when the door had closed behind the irate Colonel. " One may forgive him for having insulted Sir Harry, though perhaps it would have been better form to wait until they were both out in the street; but I don't know what right he had to be so rude to us."

"He wasn't rude," answered Muriel rather sadly, for she felt sure that her friend would now be her friend no longer—" he was only offended, and he had a right to be that. We ought not to receive Sir Harry Brewster; I have thought so all along."

" Papa doesn't think so, it seems," returned

Sylvia, preparing herself for battle ; " nor does Lady Morecambe. What have we to do with the sins which our acquaintances may have committed in days gone by ? I suppose that even Colonel Medhurst, if he were put into the confessional, would have to plead guilty to a few peccadilloes."

But Muriel declined the fray. She reserved what she had to say for her brother, with whom she sought an interview in his study before she went to bed and to whom she gave an account of the afternoon's events.

" Dear me, what an odd coincidence," remarked Mr. Wentworth, after patiently hearing her out. " Now that you mention it, I think I do recollect that the lady's maiden name was Medhurst. Well, of course we mustn't let these two fire-eaters come to fisticuffs here. You had better give the necessary orders to the servants."

"I doubt whether Colonel Medhurst will ever come here again," answered Muriel : "I am sure he won't if Sir Harry Brewster is to be admitted. Surely there can be no question as to which of them ought to have the door shut against him."

An unwelcome idea was suggested to Mr. Wentworth by this speech. He had always taken the possibility of Muriel's marriage into account, but only in the same sense as he had contemplated the possibility of the house being burnt down or of his own premature demise. Just as there are a good many non-marrying men, so one occasionally comes across a non-marrying woman. He had mentally included his sister in the latter restricted class, and it is needless to add that he had done so very willingly. She was free to marry if she pleased, only her marriage would mean the curtailment of a considerable proportion of his personal comforts ; and that may have been one reason why he at once jumped to the conclusion that Colonel Medhurst was in no way worthy of her.

" I am not prepared to shut my door against anybody," he rejoined rather sharply ; " but supposing, for the sake of argument, that I had to be so uncivil, I would rather turn my back upon Medhurst, who is simply a heavy nonentity, than upon Sir Harry Brewster, who is a man of the world and a pleasant companion."

Muriel declined to take up the cudgels on Colonel Medhurst's behalf.

" I daresay you would," she replied : " but why will you persist in shutting your eyes to the fact that you are not the only person in the house ? It isn't for your sake or for Colonel Medhurst's, but for Sylvia's, that I want you to put a stop to this intimacy with Sir Harry Brewster."

Mr. Wentworth laughed.

"One of the funniest things about women," he remarked, "is the obstinacy with which they cling to an idea when there is not a tittle of evidence to support it. I have had more oppor- tunities of seeing Sylvia and Sir Harry together than you have, and if you will believe me—but of course you won't—neither of them is dream- ing of a project which is palpably inadmissible. I grant you that Sir Harry treated his wife abominably; but, as she was not a relation of mine, I don't feel called upon to avenge her wrongs. Colonel Medhurst naturally does. Very well; let him avenge them in any way that may recommend itself to him. If cutting our acquaintance is one of them, I shall submit uncomplainingly."

"You don't think it worth while to shield Sylvia from the risk of a great misfortune then ? "

"My dear Muriel, haven't I just told you that

the risk has no existence, except in your imagination? If you will only leave Sylvia alone, and give her time, she will probably end by marrying Johnny Hill. She won't marry Sir Harry Brewster for two good reasons. Firstly, he won't ask her, and secondly, I shouldn't allow her to accept him if he did. Colonel Medhurst and he must settle their differences between them ; only, as I said before, I should take measures, if I were you, to prevent a settlement from occurring in this house. Our obvious course is to remain neutral."

Muriel sighed and left the room. She could do nothing with this selfish optimist ; but she inwardly registered a vow to the effect that if Sir Harry Brewster had the effrontery to call again, he should find neither her nor Sylvia at home.

CHAPTER XI.

IT is not with impunity that a sober, middle-
aged man can permit his passions to gain the
mastery over him. In the inevitable reaction
which ensues, his self-esteem is sure to sink to a
very low ebb, and he not only feels that he has
behaved like a fool, but is apt to conclude that
he has been inexcusable in so behaving. So, in
spite of the unbending attitude which Colonel
Medhurst had assumed on taking leave of Miss
Wentworth, he had not proceeded far on his
homeward way before the voice of his conscience
began to make itself heard. Nothing—so he
said to himself—can justify a fracas in the

presence of ladies, and if an actual fracas had been averted, the credit was due to Sir Harry Brewster, not to him. For two pins he would have caught the man by the throat or knocked him down. He shuddered as he inwardly made that acknowledgment, and told himself that he was no better than a vulgar ruffian. Of course, what he ought to have done, on hearing who the stranger was, was simply to go away. At the most, he might perhaps have explained his reasons for doing so in a few words.

But it was too late to think of that now. What he had done could not be undone, and he must accept the consequences. One of these certainly seemed to be that a coldness would arise between him and the woman whom he no longer disguised from himself that he loved, and another, he supposed, would be that he must make some appointment to meet Sir Harry

Brewster. That the man deserved to be insulted did not alter the fact that he had insulted him ; he could not very well refuse to take any further notice of one whom he had treated in that way.

At the same time he did not, now that his head was less hot, see what satisfaction either of them was likely to obtain from a meeting. It was all very well to talk about thrashing Sir Harry ; but such things, if they are to be done at all, must be done upon the spur of the moment, and pistol and rapier have fallen into disuse in this country. Under the circumstances, therefore, nothing could be exchanged between him and his enemy except abusive language, which was scarcely a fit method of fighting for men to adopt. More mature reflection, how-ever, led him to believe that there was, after all, just a possibility of some good resulting from the proposed interview. Remembering what

Muriel had told him about her uneasiness re-
specting her niece, it dawned upon him that the
undesirable suitor of whom she had spoken
could be no other than Sir Harry Brewster,
and he immediately made up his mind that he
would at least relieve her of that source of
anxiety. That it was in his power to do this
he felt little doubt. It was not in his power to
do anything for his sister; if he killed Sir Harry
she would be none the better off, nor would she
thank him. Her injuries were irremediable;
but surely, knowing what he did, he could bring
pressure enough to bear upon this scoundrel to
preserve an innocent girl from sharing her fate?
He had the simplicity to imagine that a threat
of exposure would suffice; for, although nothing
was more probable than that the man would
tell Miss Wentworth a tissue of lies, these could
easily be proved to be lies by the production of
a file of old newspapers.

14*

The outcome of his meditations was that, as soon as he had dined, he despatched the following telegram to the address given him by Sir Harry Brewster :

" Shall I find you at home at eleven o'clock to-morrow ? "

Telegraphing had the double advantage of insuring a speedy answer and obviating all necessity for conventional forms of epistolatory politeness. Sir Harry's reply was not long in reaching him.

" Glad to see you at the hour named."

" I wish I could make you sorry to see me, you villain ! " muttered the Colonel, grinding his teeth, as he tossed the slip of paper into the fire. " Ah, if only you and I had lived a hundred years ago ! "

But one must needs conform to the usages of
the period to which one belongs, and an English-
man in the latter part of the nineteenth century
has no means of healing his wounded honour
save such as a court of law may be pleased to
accord to him.   Colonel Medhurst, therefore,
presented himself at Queen Anne's Mansions, on
the following morning, like any ordinary visitor,
and was admitted as soon as the hall-porter had
ascertained that Sir Harry Brewster was out of
bed.

It was in Queen Anne's Mansions that Sir
Harry Brewster resided at this time, his family
mansion in Grosvenor Square having been let
for a term of years owing to unavoidable
circumstances.   The suite of apartments which
he occupied formed very comfortable bachelor's
quarters, nor would anyone have supposed, on
seeing them, that their owner was suffering from
financial straits.   Their owner, clad in a crimson

plush smoking-suit, had finished his breakfast and was enjoying a cigarette and the perusal of *The Sportsman*, when the grim Colonel was announced. He at once got up.

"I really don't know whether it is any use to ask you to sit down," he said ; "but pray do so if you feel inclined. In fact, you may consider me entirely at your orders. I am ready to give you a cigar or to clear away the furniture and engage in a stand-up fight — just as you please."

"I came here," answered Medhurst, speaking in the sharp, *staccato* accents of a man who has some difficulty in controlling himself, " because, after what I said to you at Miss Wentworth's house yesterday, it seemed to me that I was bound to accept your invitation to meet you alone. It is for you to decide whether there shall be a stand-up fight or not. For my own part, I don't propose to break your bones, because I don't see what would be the good of it."

Sir Harry smiled. " You are a heavier man than I, Colonel Medhurst," he remarked; "but, lest you should think that I am afraid of you, I may mention that I know how to use my fists about as well as any man in England. I doubt whether you would get a chance of breaking any of my bones in two hours. Besides which, I agree with you that there would be no particular good in it if you did. Well, what can I do for you? You consider that I treated your sister badly and I do not deny it. Would you like me to cross the Channel and fight a duel with you? If so, I'm quite willing to oblige you."

" No," answered the other gloomily ; " I don't see that there would be any good in that either. And why should I let you have a shot at me ? I meant what I told you yesterday ; you are not a gentleman and you have no title to be treated as one."

"From the reason which you gave just now for your visit," returned Sir Harry, without losing his temper, " I supposed that you wished to give me an opportunity of avenging an insult. If you didn't, and if you won't fight, may I venture to ask why you are here ? "

The question was certainly excusable ; but Medhurst, who had not expected it to be put quite so soon, was not prepared to answer it forthwith. He gnawed his moustache for a moment, and then remarked :

"You don't deny having treated my sister badly ; but, in my opinion, 'badly' is scarcely a strong enough word to use. As much as that might have been said if you had at least kept your hands off her ; but to beat a defenceless woman is—well, it is simply to put yourself outside the pale of common humanity."

"On my side," replied Sir Harry, "I may say that 'beating' is too strong a word to use. I will tell you exactly what happened. Your sister is a pious woman, and, like many other pious women, she has the gift of exasperating sinners beyond all bearing. She so exasperated me by accusing me of misconduct in the presence of the servants, that one evening I took her by the shoulders and pushed her out of the dining-room. On another occasion when her maid was in the room, she came close up to me and poured out a torrent of abuse against a woman of whom she was jealous and whom she mentioned by name. I was angry with her for mentioning names; I threw up my hand rather with the intention of waving her back than of touching her, and I certainly did hit her on the arm. The maid afterwards swore that I had boxed her ears—which was a lie. Mind you, I admit that I was violent and I admit that my wife had

reason to be jealous; only I submit that when
you speak of my having beaten her, you go too
far."

"There is the evidence of eye-witnesses,
which was not refuted and which was believed
by the jury," returned Medhurst doggedly; "I
am not bound to accept your version of what
occurred. I don't care to discuss the matter;
it is past mending. But one thing I wish to say
to you: you must cease your visits to Miss
Wentworth's house. It has come to my knowledge that you are paying attention to her niece
—a girl who is scarcely more than a child—
and you can't suppose that I shall allow that
to go on. Even you ought to feel that such
attentions on your part are a little too in-
famous."

"I have been very forbearing with you,
Colonel Medhurst," answered Sir Harry; "I
have tried to make every allowance for the

indignation which you express, and which I should express quite as forcibly, I daresay, if I were in your place. But I must point out to you that you are now putting forward claims which are wholly inadmissible. Naturally, I am not going to tell you whether you are mistaken or not in imagining that I am paying attentions to Miss Sylvia Wentworth; but, if I were, I could not recognise any right on your part to interfere with me. We will drop that subject, if you please."

" Then I shall direct Mr. Wentworth's attention to the report of the proceedings instituted against you in the Divorce Court."

"Of course you are at liberty to do so ; although I presume that he is already acquainted with them. Possibly, if I think fit to make the attempt, I may convince him that the evidence was not strictly in accordance with the facts."

"Possibly you may, if you are shameless enough—as perhaps you are. And yet it does seem to me that no human being with a spark of manliness left in him could be quite such a rascal. Surely it is no great thing to ask that you should refrain from bringing misery upon a girl who isn't old enough to understand what a history like yours means! You have escaped scot-free; nobody has punished you for what you have done; as I have told you, I myself don't intend to punish you——"

"Oh, excuse me," interrupted Sir Harry; "you really must not expect me to thank you for sparing me. I have offered to give you any kind of satisfaction that you like to ask for; if you won't take advantage of my offer the fault is not mine. Upon no conceivable ground are you entitled to dictate to me who my friends shall be."

There was no disputing that assertion, and Colonel Medhurst, after a moment of meditation, realised that he could not dispute it. "Very well," he said; "you will take your course, and I shall take mine. I don't think so badly of Mr. Wentworth as to believe that he will let you into his house when he has heard what I shall tell him about you."

With that he turned on his heel and left his antagonist, feeling that he had by no means had the best of the encounter.

And now it seemed to him to be nothing less than his simple duty to call in Upper Brook Street and make a more ample apology to Miss Wentworth for his treatment of her visitor than he had made at the time. He had been in the right so far as Sir Harry Brewster was concerned, but he had certainly been in the wrong in creating an embarrassing situation for a lady, and he felt that he ought to say so. Per-

haps he may also have been influenced by a
strong desire to make his peace with the
lady in question ; but if so, he was honestly
unconscious of it.   Towards five o'clock,
therefore,   he   wended   his   way   westwards,
animated by sentiments of the most penitent
humility.

Now,   it   so   chanced   that   at   the   same
hour   Muriel   was   returning   home   from   her
daily   visit   to   the   children's   hospital,   and
thus it was that she was overtaken within a
few   yards   of   her   own   door   by   a   gentleman
whose   aspect   was   very   much   less   warlike
than   it   had   been   on   the   occasion   of   their
last meeting.

Medhurst   offered   his   excuses   a   little
awkwardly, yet after a fashion which was
neither unflattering nor displeasing to their
recipient.   She understood very well that he
could   not   bring   himself   to   express   regret   for

having used plain language to a scoundrel, but that he was mortally afraid lest, by so doing, he should have lost the good opinion of one whose friendship he valued, and she hastened to assure him that there was no ground for that apprehension.

"You could not have acted in any other way," she declared; "you only said what it was impossible to help saying, and I quite agree with you that Sir Harry Brewster ought not to be allowed to enter our house. But what can I do? It is not my house, and my brother laughs at the idea of my setting myself up as a judge of the morality of his acquaintances."

"It isn't as an acquaintance of your brother's that you object to Sir Harry Brewster," remarked Medhurst, unwittingly taking up a somewhat more peremptory tone than he would have adopted, had he been reproached for his indiscretion. " I won't pretend to be ignorant of what is so obvious, and it is difficult to me to believe that Mr. Wentworth can be ignorant of it either."

" He can always manage to shut his eyes to things which he doesn't wish to see," sighed Muriel. " I have told him what I am afraid of ; but he treats it as a mare's nest. He doesn't want to cut Sir Harry Brewster, who amuses him, and he refuses to believe that there can be any danger in the case of a man who is almost as old as he himself is."

" But even admitting that there is no danger, he must see that his daughter ought not to be upon intimate terms with a man of that character. I think, if you don't mind, I will have a little talk with him upon the subject."

" Of course I don't mind," answered Muriel, " but I am afraid he will only laugh at you. I have told the servants I shall not be at home to Sir Harry Brewster in future. That much I was entitled to do; but I can't prevent Sylvia from meeting him elsewhere. Fortunately she will be going down to the country in a few days, and I have written to beg Harriet Morecambe to keep her as long as possible. I don't think Sir Harry is serious: it is about her that I am frightened."

In speaking with so much frankness Muriel was giving Colonel Medhurst a proof of friendship which he appreciated and which gladdened his heart.

"We ought to be able to protect your niece between us, Miss Wentworth," said he, confidently. "Brazen it out as he may, that rascal must be ashamed of himself and must know that he hasn't a leg to stand upon. Anyhow, I'm glad to think that he won't be received by you any more. Probably Mr. Wentworth has forgotten some incidents of which I shall take the liberty to remind him."

Muriel, who by this time was standing on the doorstep, smiled and looked doubtfully at him. "You won't be angry if you are politely requested to mind your own business, will you?" she asked.

"Not I! I consider it my business to be of use to you in any way that I can—and I don't lose my temper very easily, Miss Wentworth, though I did forget myself in your presence yesterday."

Muriel smiled again and held out her hand. "I won't ask you to come in this evening," said she, "because I think perhaps you had better not meet Sylvia; but if you care to call in a few days you can do so without any fear of finding Sir Harry Brewster in the drawing-room."

So the day ended for Colonel Medhurst a good deal better than it had begun. With what

weapons he was to defeat the machinations ot
Sir Harry Brewster he hardly knew ; but one
thing was, happily, beyond doubt, namely, that
he had entered into an alliance with Muriel
Wentworth.

CHAPTER XII.

"Oh, by the way, Harriet," said Lord More-cambe, bustling into his wife's boudoir with a great show of haste, "I have just had a tele-gram which concerns you rather more than me. I suppose the house isn't quite chock full, is it?"

Lady Morecambe pushed her chair back from the table at which she was writing letters and looked sharply at the speaker, whose eyes dropped somewhat guiltily under her gaze. She knew very well that when her husband pretended to be in a hurry it was because he was afraid of being scolded, and although in a general way she was the most good-natured and accommodating of wives, there were certain pre-rogatives of hers to which she clung tenaciously.

One of these was the right to say who should and who should not be invited to Morecambe Priory—a very necessary privilege to insist upon, owing to the indiscriminate hospitality of her lord and master, who, had he been allowed to do as he pleased, would have asked all sorts of impossible people to stay with him upon the plea that they were what he called " good fellows."

" I can't say whether the house is full or not until I have seen the telegram," she replied ; " give it to me."

But Lord Morecambe did not seem disposed to part at once with the slip of paper which he held in his hand. " Oh, it's only from Brewster," he said, in a deprecating tone of voice. " Wants to come down for the ball to-night. Rather cool, I admit, but that's just his way, you know. Of course you don't like him ; but really he won't trouble you much this time. One more or less

among such a crowd of people can't make any
great difference, can it ? "

A very angry woman was Lady Morecambe
when the name of this self-invited guest was re-
vealed to her.

" I never heard of such impudence in my
life ! " she exclaimed. " Most certainly the
house is full—and if it was empty there would
be no room in it for Sir Harry Brewster. You
had better telegraph to him at once and say so.
I could believe anything of the man's impertinence, but I do think he might have known better
than to imagine that he could make a cat's paw
of me in such an open way. And really it is too
bad of Sylvia Wentworth. They must have
arranged it between them. Muriel cannot have
any suspicion, because she wrote to me a day or
two ago, begging me to keep Sylvia here as long
as possible, and hinting that she wanted the girl
to be removed from London on account of some

flirtation or entanglement. It is easy enough to guess who the man must be. Well, he is very much mistaken if he thinks he can use this house as a place of assignation."

"Oh, come," expostulated Lord Morecambe ; " I'm sure you can't mean to accuse a child like poor little Sylvia of doing such naughty things. As for Brewster, his flirtations have always been with married women, you know. Besides, he has turned over a new leaf of late, I'm told. I don't see what chance he can have had of making assignations with Sylvia Wentworth either. In all probability he hasn't set eyes on her since they met here."

" Unfortunately, that is just what he has ; I have heard of it from more than one quarter during the last few days. Sir Harry was seen driving Sylvia and her father on a coach, and they were at the theatre together too, and some- where else—at Richmond, I think."

"O, well, there you are!" said Lord Morecambe, with an air of relief. "If the girl's
father allows Brewster to go about with her
—and really I don't know why he shouldn't—
it's none of our business to take precautions."

"I know very little of Mr. Wentworth," remarked Lady Morecambe; "he may be a
perfect fool, and I dare say he is—nine men
out of ten are. But you may depend upon it
that he will have sense enough to abuse me if
Sylvia gets into trouble, and I don't choose to
lay myself open to justifiable abuse. Sir Harry
Brewster doesn't cross this threshold—that much
I can promise you."

"But, my dear," said Lord Morecambe,
timidly putting forward a consideration which
he had hoped would have suggested itself to her
ladyship, "how is the thing to be helped? You
see, he must have started by this time, and it really
is impossible to turn a man away from one's door."

Lady Morecambe replied resolutely that this was not only possible but that it should be done. It was not her fault if every bedroom in the house was occupied, nor was she bound to prove that such was the case. "We don't keep an inn," she said.

"No; but Judkins at the 'Morecambe Arms' does," remarked her husband. "Of course Brewster will go there, and of course he will turn up at the ball to-night. We can't refuse to admit him without having a regular row—which would be deuced unpleasant for everybody."

Lady Morecambe was constrained to admit that a regular row was certainly undesirable, and, after a few minutes of meditation, she decided that house-room had better be given to Sir Harry Brewster for the night. "He shall leave by the first train to-morrow morning, though," she declared; "if you don't tell him

that, I will. And you may give him to understand at the same time that he will never be
asked here again, in the shooting season or out
of it. Of all the wicked things that he has
done, it does seem to me that this is the worst
and the most selfish. Women who have been
out in the world for half a dozen years can take
care of themselves; but no man who was not an
absolute wretch would try to break a schoolgirl's
heart for the sake of securing a few hours of
amusement."

Lady Morecambe was perhaps justified in accusing Sir Harry of abnormal selfishness, for he
was in truth as selfish a man as ever lived; yet
it so happened that in this particular instance
he did not deserve the censure passed upon him.
He had not attempted to amuse himself with
Sylvia Wentworth; he had not flirted with her;
but, by one of those odd strokes of fate against
which age and wisdom afford no protection, he

had fallen desperately in love with the girl. At
the outset, as has been said, he had thought of
her probable fortune as an acquisition which
might be worth making a bid for, but of late
he had put all such mercenary considerations
away from him. He would have been willing to
marry her if she had not had a penny, nor the
prospect of one, and his only dread was that her
family would never consent to her union with a
divorced man. After the little scene which had
taken place between him and Colonel Medhurst,
it was of course his first duty to make out some
sort of a case for himself with Mr. Wentworth,
and he had hesitated for some time before
despatching the telegram which had so greatly
incensed Lady Morecambe. Eventually, however, he had made up his mind to be present at
the ball. For one thing, he had promised Sylvia
that he would be there, and for another, he persuaded himself that he owed an explanation to

her rather than to anybody else. He was fully aware that he would not be made welcome by Lady Morecambe ; but that did not disturb him in the least. He took care to preclude the possibility of her shutting her door in his face, and, as he did not propose to remain more than one night under her roof, he was able to contemplate the prospect of a cold reception with philosophic indifference.

Sylvia, meanwhile, was exercised by grave doubts as to whether Sir Harry would put in an appearance or not. She had expected to hear, directly or indirectly, of him before she left London ; but, since he had made no sign, she was not free from anxiety lest the redoubtable Colonel Medhurst should have scared him away. She did not realise what that anxiety meant ; she was not conscious of being ready to forgive him for any iniquity that he might have perpetrated in the past ; all she knew was that if

he deserted her, her life would once more become as dull and empty as it had been in the
old days which already seemed so far away,
and against that outlook she rebelled with all
the passionate petulance of a spoilt child. But
in the course of the afternoon her fears were
dissipated, for she knew that Sir Harry was
coming. Lady Morecambe, who had hitherto
been amiability itself, looked so annoyed and
spoke so snappishly to her that she could form
a pretty shrewd guess at what had occurred,
and it was without any surprise that she heard
herself addressed, just before dinner, in a voice
which had become both familiar and sweet to
her ears.

"May I be allowed to book two consecutive
dances?" asked Sir Harry hurriedly. "As you
may imagine, I want to speak to you, and it is
not likely that I shall be granted an opportunity
before the dancing has begun."

"I will give you four and five," answered Sylvia, who had already possessed herself of a programme. "Are we to sit them both out? If so, perhaps you would like to have another one later on."

"I must leave that to your generosity; I don't know whether you will be inclined to dance with me later on. I suppose it will depend upon whether you are satisfied or not with what I have to say to you."

This was all that passed between them; for now Lady Morecambe abruptly put a stop to their colloquy by leading Sylvia away to the other end of the room. But nobody knew better than Lady Morecambe that it is impossible in a ball-room to separate two people who are bent upon coming together. She did what she could; she kept Sylvia beside her until the guests began to arrive; she introduced more young men to her *protégée* than there were dances on the programme, but she could not erase Sir Harry's Brewster's name from the card which was attached to Miss Sylvia's fan, nor did her duties as a hostess permit her to quit her post in the doorway.

And so it came to pass that when the band struck up the opening bars of the fourth dance Sylvia, on Sir Harry Brewster's arm, was being conducted out of the ball-room into an adjacent conservatory, where comfortable seats and subdued light and privacy were obtainable by those in search of such advantages.

"I am going to tell you nothing but the truth," he began, plunging at once and without preface into the midst of the subject of which they were both thinking. "If I don't tell you the whole truth, you will understand that it is because some things can't be put into plain words. That man Medhurst had a right to call me all the bad names in the dictionary; his sister had a right to divorce me, and all I have to say for myself is that I was never guilty of physical violence against her, except in a technical sense. She was one of those good women who make everybody about her miserable. She made me miserable, and I have no doubt that I made her miserable. The fact is that I hated her. Perhaps I might be able to show that there were some excuses for me, though I don't pretend that they were sufficient excuses; but, before I attempt to do that, I should like to ask you whether, after what I have admitted, you can possibly continue to treat me as a friend."

Sylvia made the answer which his knowledge of her character may have led him to expect.

" I don't make it a condition that my friends should be saints," she said; "as a rule I don't like saints. I think I can understand that there were excuses for you; but really I would rather hear no more about it. It is all over and done with, and—and I daresay you are sorry. Only I wish that your—your enemy were anybody but Colonel Medhurst!"

"You are very kind, and very generous," answered Sir Harry; "but why do you say that? Is Colonel Medhurst a more formidable enemy than any other man could be?"

"Yes; because Muriel believes in him, and, although she isn't exactly mistress of the house, she can close it against visitors whom she doesn't choose to see. She has given orders that you are not to be let in again; I know that from my maid, who was told by the butler."

"If it had depended upon you, then, that order wouldn't have been given?"

"No; it wouldn't. What have I to do with Colonel Medhurst and his grievances? And why should I deprive myself of one of the very few friends I have in the world?"

Sir Harry's rejoinder was somewhat startling, and in truth he himself had not contemplated coming to the point quite so soon ; but such success as he had had in life had been chiefly due to audacity, and he had acquired an instinctive knack of striking while the iron was hot.

" Shall I tell you something ? " said he. " Circumstances will never admit of my being your friend. I must be more than that or nothing at all."

And as she drew back with a half-frightened look and made no answer, he went on : " I know it is ridiculous for a man of my age to flatter himself that he can obtain what he might have hoped for twenty years ago, and even if I were younger, I should be heavily handicapped by the events that you have been told of. Nevertheless, I can but say that I love you with all my heart and soul. Now give me the *coup de grâce* quickly and put me out of my misery."

Sylvia was taken by surprise ; yet if ample time for deliberation had been accorded to her her reply would, no doubt, have been the same. She had not until that moment been aware that she loved Sir Harry Brewster ; but she was aware of it now, and that being so, it was neither his age nor his history that could deter her from answering :

" I can't send you away ; I—I care too much for you. There will be a terrible fuss about it ; but—I don't mind, if you don't."

What followed was what presumably always does follow a declaration of that nature. Lady Morecambe, released by the lateness of the hour from the task of shaking hands with a multitude of people whose names she could not recollect, and noticing with alarm that neither Sir Harry Brewster nor Sylvia Wentworth were in the ball-room, reached the conservatory just in time to discover the former in the very act of embracing the latter. Wrath and dismay rendered her speechless for an instant; but only for an instant.

"Sir Harry," she exclaimed, advancing with rapid steps upon the delinquents, "you are worse than wicked! I will never forgive you for this —never. If you have an atom of honourable feeling left you will at least keep silence about what has happened; but I am afraid your honour would be a broken reed to lean upon. You will be so good as to leave us now and to go away by the first train to-morrow morning."

"I will go away to-night, if you like, Lady Morecambe," answered Sir Harry composedly. "All the same, I don't quite understand what you are so angry about."

"You don't understand!" returned the irate lady; "you don't understand that you have committed an abominable outrage. But of course you do understand, and I have nothing more

to say to you. Please leave Miss Wentworth
to me."

Sir Harry bowed, smiled slightly and retired,
throwing a reassuring glance back at Sylvia, who
thereupon observed:

"I think it is you who do not understand,
Lady Morecambe. Sir Harry Brewster and I
are engaged to be married."

"Oh, you foolish child! Don't you know that
the man has a wife living?"

"I know that he once had a wife, and that he
is divorced from her."

"Good Heavens! what is the world coming
to? In my young days some people used to
call me fast; but I am sure I never could have
spoken of divorce in that cool way. You must
have taken leave of your senses, Sylvia. Well, I
am not responsible; I neither asked nor wished
Sir Harry to come here, and I wash my hands
of the whole business. To-morrow I shall send

you home to your father, who, I hope and trust,
will have the decency not to. blame me for a
catastrophe which I have had no share in
bringing about."

" I will take the whole blame upon myself,
Lady Morecambe," answered Sylvia submissively
but firmly. " I know I shall have a bad time of
it, and I don't care. Papa may forbid me to
marry Sir Harry Brewster now; but I shall
marry him as soon as I am of age."

Lady Morecambe was a little staggered. She
had not been prepared for the girl's quiet determination, which she was unable to shake by a
brief but vivid sketch of Sir Harry's career. The
fact was that Sylvia had all her life been accustomed to impose her will upon those about her,
and it was not likely that her self-confidence
should desert her in so important a crisis as this.
She was happy and she was triumphant ; in her
heart she was persuaded that Sir Harry had

never loved anyone but her, and if she thought
at all of the woman who had been his wife, it was
only with a sort of contemptuous pity.

Before the evening was over she contrived to
exchange a few more words with him. She was
returning home on the following day, she said,
and she would of course communicate the news
of her engagement at once to her people. Perhaps he had better not call until he heard from
her.

" I will do just what you tell me," Sir Harry
replied. " We must make up our minds to a
good deal of opposition, you know."

"Oh yes ; there will be opposition at first.
But they will give in after a time—they must.
Even if they succeed in separating us for years—
but there is very little fear of their doing that—I
shall not change. Will you ? "

He said what everybody else would have said
in his place and said it with as much sincerity as

anybody else could have felt. Like Lady Morecambe, he was astonished at Sylvia's calm deci·
sion of purpose, and, unlike her, he was touched
by it. If it were true that a reformed rake makes
the best husband, there would perhaps have been
no great reason to pity that self-willed and inexperienced young woman ; but in all probability
it is not true. At any rate, a man of Sir Harry
Brewster's age is not much more likely to make
a fresh start than habitual criminals are to earn
an honest livelihood, and it may have been some
dim perception of this fact that caused him to
sigh in the moment of victory.

END OF VOL. I.